DEVIANT

NATASHA KNIGHT

1

JULIEN

I'd been watching her for the last three days.

I didn't know what it was I found so appealing about the girl. She was a sneaky little peeping Tom.

Maybe it was her pretty green eyes, or how wide they grew at the things she watched us do. At the things I made the girl whose ass I was currently fucking do.

Regardless, her fate was sealed the moment she pushed the curtains aside and saw my face.

No witnesses, no matter what. That was rule number one. It had to be.

She hadn't yet realized I'd seen her, that she was being watched as she herself was doing the watching. Her attention was fully absorbed by the fucking.

But I studied her face, saw her mouth open, her little pink tongue dart out to lick those full lips, her throat work as she swallowed hard, her cheeks flushing a deep red.

Her face imprinted on my mind. I'd recognize her anywhere now. It was one of the things I was so good at. A blessing and a curse all at once. Never forget a face. Never forget their eyes, how they change when they realize what's happening, when terror grips them.

Forgetting was a gift.

People spent their lives chasing the past, trying to hold on to something long gone. Desperate to remember.

Me? I wished I could forget.

It had been three days since she'd first seen us. I was sure it was by accident, or at least it had been the first time.

Her room was situated directly across the courtyard of the cheap little hotel. She'd pulled the curtains apart to open her window when she'd stumbled upon the sight of us fucking.

I'd ducked my head out of sight, and wouldn't have thought much of it, but when, a moment later, the small hand pulled the curtains just a little wider, just wide enough to see, my curiosity had gotten the best of me.

It had been her face. It was just so innocent, so... corruptible. Irresistible to a man like me.

I always liked to play with them first, fuck with them a little. It was cruel, reprehensible, really. I knew it, but it didn't make me enjoy it any less.

The blonde began to squirm beneath me, almost stealing my attention from the woman in the window. I glanced down at her, at the mass of dyed hair spilling over her back, mascara smeared across her face, her mouth open. I looked at her ass, at my cock disappearing inside it.

She'd been a good fuck, but this would be the last time. Three days was long enough. I had a job to do, after all, and the girl in the window would already delay me. I couldn't exactly assassinate my mark in front of her. She'd freak out, and that was more attention than I needed.

Gripping the blonde's hair tightly, I tugged hard, giving her a grin she likely thought a smile before pushing her face into the mattress to shut her up.

She mewled and I rubbed her clit with my free hand, turning that sound into something else. Pain and pleasure, pleasure and pain. They never knew which it was; there was never any clear line for them.

With the blonde's face buried in the blankets, I studied my little voyeur. She was still there, still watching — but her hand had disappeared into her pants. I'd make her show me just what those fingers were doing when the time came.

That made me grin, but when she looked up and her green gaze met mine, I could almost hear her gasp at the shock of being caught.

It was then my grin widened into something else, something meant to scare.

I gripped the blonde's hips, all while daring the woman who watched to draw the curtains closed, to turn away. I fucked the woman before me then, really fucked her, and just before I came inside that tight ass, my little voyeur blinked as if coming out of a trance, her face going bright red before she pulled the curtains tight.

My low growl made the blonde look over her shoulder. I met her gaze, my own hardening as I forced myself to remember who she was, the things she'd done, and the job I still had to do.

That part always made my cock harder.

Any person with morals would probably worry about that, about liking this sort of work, but I had never claimed to have any of those. Or if I had, they'd been beaten out of me years ago. That was what made me so good at my job.

I looked down at her asshole, at my cock as it plunged

deep, knowing I hurt and gave pleasure at once, not caring which was the dominant of the two as I exploded inside her. But when I closed my eyes, it was the voyeur's eyes I saw, not the woman who had my cock buried inside her.

If only the bitch before me knew how lucky she was. She'd just been granted an extra day to live.

2

MIA

I had to remind myself there were worse things than being on the run, and certainly worse things than being on the run in southern Italy. The waiter set my espresso down, momentarily interrupting my thoughts, which wasn't a bad thing.

What had I been thinking watching them? Watching *him*? Was I so hard up?

I covered my face in shame.

Well, I couldn't *not* watch. He was incredibly good looking for one thing, blue eyes, dark hair, scruff along his jaw, and a grin that was wicked, devious even. I imagined he was a man who didn't hear the word no very often, at least not from women.

Then there was his body. Big, cut with muscle and heavily tattooed. That last part intrigued me while scaring the crap out of me.

There was something about him, something about the ink covering most of his chest and arms. I just knew that for someone like him, it wasn't about vanity. Each of those tattoos meant something.

Watching him fuck her the way he had? All I had to do was imagine it was me on my knees before him and I came. Hard.

This had been going on for the last three days. I'd been spying — to my utter disgrace — on the couple in the hotel room across the courtyard as they made love.

No, wait. There was no love making that I could see. He'd been fucking her. And I'd stood there like a perverted — and horny — peeping Tom unable to look away. And today, he'd caught me.

I groaned, ashamed, rubbed my temples, then picked up my coffee and took a sip. This wouldn't do, I needed something stronger.

The waiter walked by and I ordered a shot of vodka, tossing it down when he brought it, looking around at the noisy little café. This was my favorite neighborhood spot and I began to recognize the regulars here.

Some part of me longed for that familiarity for myself, even if it was an impossibility, given the circumstances of my stay in Italy.

I'd been in the city of Cosenza for six weeks now, had rented one of the small studio apartments the hotel offered for long-term guests. I'd been hopping from city to city for the last year and I was tired.

I missed home more than I thought I would. Well, not home so much as my friends, but when you testify against your stepbrother, the son of a man whose family has earned their fortune on the suffering of others, and put him away for a good chunk of his life, you can't exactly go back.

I wasn't even sure if stepbrother was the right term. My sister, Tanya, who had practically raised me since I was five, had married Samuel St. Rose when I was thirteen, and she was eighteen. He was in his mid-forties. Jason and Allison were Samuel's kids from his previous marriage. Although technically the term stepbrother and stepsister didn't work, given our ages, it was what I called them. Never mind the fact that Tanya was just a year older than Jason.

My sister had known all along what Samuel St. Rose did for a living. She'd married him anyway, and I understood that.

We'd come from nothing. He had everything.

And on top of that, she had fallen in love with him. I think it was Tanya who had been the most surprised at that. We'd lived on the street for stretches of time on two separate occasions. She was tough as nails. Samuel changed that, and in a way, I was at least glad for that part of things. Glad that in her short life, she had had at least that.

My friendship with Allison, my stepsister, was another one of the good things that came out of this. And truly, Samuel had been kind to me. Had treated me like his own kid. He did it for Tanya, I knew that. He had loved her. But when everything had happened, he had chosen his son over me. I wasn't his by blood, and he'd do whatever he had to do to protect his son. Even if he knew that son didn't deserve his protection.

I didn't realize my sister had been trying to protect me until it was too late.

Ironically, I received her letter on the same day as I received news of her death. She'd tried to call me twice that week, but I'd been too busy to talk to her. Maybe if I had, she would have told me what had happened, what she'd been thinking about doing. Maybe I could have helped her. She'd been scared and I hadn't known it. And when Samuel had found out what she'd done, all bets were off. Suddenly, he wasn't so nice to me, and between him and Jason, I knew the danger I was in. It was then I'd decided to go to the police, to tell what Jason, my stepbrother, had done to me, what he had done to my sister. Tell them what kind of man he really was. Tell it before he hurt anyone else.

But by doing that, by going against him, I'd gone against the family and broken a promise I'd never wanted to make.

When Jason ended up in prison, he vowed revenge, and I believed him. Samuel wasn't as reckless as Jason, but what I saw in his eyes the day his son was sentenced scared me to death. I received a promise that I'd be made to pay for my betrayal. We were family after all. Family didn't rat out family, they didn't talk about what happened behind closed doors, and certainly not after an agreement had been made and money had exchanged hands.

I scoffed at that. Family. No, we were certainly not family.

Catching the waiter's eye, I ordered another shot and drank that down too before reaching into my bag to locate my wallet. It was late, just past midnight. I'd have to go back at some point. I'd just leave the curtains drawn until the couple checked out. Surely, they'd be gone soon.

But just as I stood to leave, the door opened — and I stopped dead.

This cannot be happening.

I tried to tell myself I was mistaken, that it wasn't him. What were the chances he'd walk into the same cafe, after all?

But it was him nonetheless.

He was dressed in a dark suit. Actually, it was the first time I'd seen him dressed at all. He was taller than I had thought, but then again, I hadn't been paying attention to his height when I'd been peering between the curtains. I'd been too busy watching them fuck. His dark hair was still wet; he'd probably showered before leaving the hotel room, and now that he stood just a few feet from me, I saw that gray dusted the scruff along his jaw, making him look even more fierce now than he had when he'd been in the room across the courtyard.

He stood there, scanning the café as if he owned the place. He finally turned his gaze in my direction and when those ice blue eyes found mine, my heart took a nose-dive to my belly.

He paused, scanning me from head to toe, and when he returned his gaze to mine and the corner of his mouth curved upward, I was left without a doubt that he recognized me too.

My chest grew tight and I couldn't breathe for a minute. One word, one thought, one sensation made me shudder. It was the same thing I'd felt the moment we'd locked eyes from across the distance of the courtyard.

Danger.

He took a step in my direction, and I blinked back to life. I wasn't about to stick around, not now that he stood in the same room as me. Gripping my purse, I hustled quickly around the tables, slipped out the door and dashed into the street.

3

JULIEN

I watched Mia St. Rose practically run out of the little café, her eyes huge with surprise when she'd seen me. It had been there again, that innocence in those emerald depths, and I almost felt a pang of guilt at what I'd have to do.

Almost.

Contrary to what some believed, I didn't enjoy killing people — at least not the ones who didn't deserve to die. But I didn't know enough about Mia St. Rose to say what the hell she deserved. My belt across her ass for spying, maybe, but that was far from death.

I was about to leave the café when I saw the waiter return to her table and pick up the check. In her rush, she'd forgotten to pay. The waiter was shaking his head, muttering some words under his breath.

"How much does she owe?" I asked.

The waiter looked up at me, surprised. I took the check from his hand and handed him a bill that would more than cover her. Then, before I even acknowledged his thanks, I left the café and followed the hurried sound of her clicking heels.

I took my time though, held back far enough to conceal my presence. There was no reason for me to chase her. I knew where she was going, and I didn't intend on introducing myself. Not yet, anyway.

After I'd finished with the blonde earlier that evening, I'd figured out which room belonged to Mia and picked the lock — a ridiculously easy thing to do at many of the older, cheaper properties in the city — and figured out who she was.

When I rounded the next corner, she was almost back at the hotel. I ducked into the shadows of a building a moment before she turned to look over her shoulder, scanning the quiet street before disappearing inside. I had an uncanny feeling I may have been just one of the things she was looking out for.

But I didn't have time to think about that when my cell phone buzzed to life. Sighing, I turned the corner before pulling the phone out of my pocket. There was no need to look at the display. I knew who the caller was.

"It's almost one in the morning." I did not want to have this conversation now.

"I have a watch, Julien. Why the fuck isn't it done?" my contact said, a man I'd never met, whom I knew simply as "Cash." He sounded pissed.

"I ran into a difficulty. It'll be done tomorrow." Honestly, I had planned on finishing it tonight, but for some reason, I liked the idea of my little voyeur watching and had wanted to see her face one more time, wanted to watch those eyes.

"You thinking with your dick again?"

Bastard was right, but I wasn't about to admit it. "Fuck you. I said I'd get it done."

"What kind of difficulty?"

"Nothing I can't manage." I wondered if he heard my hesitation.

His silence told me he had. "No witnesses. You know the deal."

Yes, I knew the deal. The blonde had to die. She was a traitor, and treason warranted a penalty of death. It was just more of a sure thing to call in a guy like him to make certain justice was served rather than going through the court system.

"It'll be done within twenty-four hours."

"See that it is," Cash finished, disconnecting the call.

Just as well.

I turned to walk back to my hotel, reaching into my pocket for a cigarette. I lit it up and took one drag before tossing it onto the street. I'd been trying to quit for over a year now. No fucking discipline when it came to nicotine though. That and fucking. They were my two addictions. At least fucking was healthy.

I pulled my phone back out of my pocket and dialed Ryan. Even as the phone rang, I wasn't sure why I was doing it.

"Yeah," came his usual greeting.

"It's Julien."

"That's why I answered the phone."

I almost smiled. Ryan was young, in his early twenties, and cocky as hell, but he did a good job and he did it quietly — as long as he got paid. Fuck him with a payment though, and your shit was all over the six o'clock news.

"I need you to find out what you can about a Mia St. Rose." I pulled out the passport I'd stolen from her room. "Birthday May 24, 1991. Born in Pittsburgh, PA."

"Got it. I'll see what I can find."

"How long?"

"Few hours, unless she's hiding something."

"Call me as soon as you know."

I reached my hotel then and hung up. It was almost one in the morning and I wished I could sleep, but insomnia went hand in hand with the job.

I went up to my room and changed into workout clothes before hitting the gym. It was well-equipped and blessedly empty. No one worked out at one in the morning except for insomniacs. I went to the treadmill first. I needed to sweat, clear my head and go over the details of the kill first. Once that was done and out of the way, I could think about Mia St. Rose's pretty green eyes.

4

MIA

I wrapped my hair in a towel and checked the time. It was the middle of the night in Philadelphia but Allison worked the overnight shift at the hospital, and that was the best time to catch her. I had a feeling I should check in, and I always trusted those instincts.

I dialed the number and she picked up on the first ring. I figured she knew it was me. I always called at random times and my phone number was always blocked. It was a precaution. I trusted Allison, but didn't want to take any chances.

"Hey, Allison."

"Mia!"

"Is this a good time?"

"Yes. Good you called, actually. Jason dropped by." There was no mistaking the anxiety in her voice.

At twenty-two, Allison was two years younger than me. She knew what Jason had done — well, part of it at least. We never talked about it, and he was her brother by blood, but I sometimes got the sense that she too was afraid of him. I'd wanted her to come with me when I'd run, but she had refused. She swore he'd never hurt her. I left and I guess if I'd believed for a moment that he would harm her, I wouldn't have left without her.

"What did he want?"

"He wanted to know if I'd heard from you."

I waited for more, holding my breath.

"He checked my phone for messages, Mia."

I never left messages for exactly that reason.

"Are you okay?" I asked.

"Yeah. He won't hurt me. It's you he's looking for."

There was a long pause.

When my sister had married Jason's father, things had been fine for the first three months. That was because Jason had been away at school. When he got back home for summer vacation though, everything changed. It was like he couldn't stand either of us, as if he hated us. He was always angry, especially when he was around me.

I knew he didn't like the fact that his dad had married Tanya. If it was solely because of the age difference, I could get that — but Samuel was happy with her. Shouldn't that have been the most important thing?

I didn't care that he didn't like me. He was kind of a jerk anyway. I never thought he'd actually hurt me, but he did. When I thought about it after the fact, I realized how naïve I'd been.

Jason was sick, but I'd been the one punished for what he'd done. My sister and stepfather had decided to send me away to boarding school. I still remember how heartbroken I'd been, how betrayed I'd felt, as if my sister were choosing her husband and her new family over me. I only understood why she'd really done it after the accident.

"Where are you, Mia? Are you coming back soon?" Allison asked, bringing me back to reality.

"You know I can't tell you where I am."

"I won't tell him. I promise."

"I know you won't want to, but Jason can be persuasive. It's for your own safety. What you don't know, he can't make you tell."

"You're right. I just... I wish I could help. Do you need money? I can send it."

I shook my head. I had some money left, not a lot, but some. Enough until I got the guts to go back and claim what my sister had left me. A million dollars, according to the attorney. It became mine when I turned twenty-five, which was in a few weeks' time. Thing was, I'd have to go back to get it. It was a stipulation of the will.

"It's okay. I'll be okay. It's just a few weeks."

"Mia, how are you going to claim the money without Jason finding out?"

"I don't know. I was hoping he'd still be in prison." Which he was supposed to be. I'd been shocked when he'd been let out early. And while I'd known he kept men on me even while he was behind bars, him being out made everything more real, more frightening. "He'll never stop looking for me, will he?"

"He says all he wants is the book, and he thinks you have it. Do you?"

I closed my eyes. I didn't want to lie to Allison, but I'd meant what I said. What she didn't know, he couldn't force out of her.

"I don't have it, I've told you that before."

"My dad knows your sister stole it. She's on a security tape."

Yes, I knew that. My sister had to have known it too when she did it. And she had to have known Samuel would punish her for it. But had she deserved death? Had that been her punishment, or was her death really just an accident?

The book in question was the ledger Samuel kept, the real one, for the dry cleaning businesses he ran as cover for the service he really offered: money laundering. I guess it kind of fit — the business, and what he truly did. That book could expose a lot of people, could put a lot of people away, including both Samuel and Jason. He was involved in his father's business too.

And it was the one thing that I could still use if I ever had my back up against a wall. I wasn't going to give that up.

"I don't have it, Allison," I lied.

"Okay, Mia. I'll keep talking to him."

"What about your dad?"

"What about him?"

Allison didn't have the best relationship with her father. Neither did Jason for that matter. From the tone of her voice, that hadn't changed.

"Nothing. Never mind. I've got to go, but I'll call you in a few days. Take care, Allison. Be safe."

"You too. I miss having you around, sis."

That made me sad. I missed Allison. We'd been close for a while.

"I miss *being* around," I said. "I'll call again soon."

After hanging up, I went to the window, drawing one curtain partially back, looking through the sheets of falling rain at the window across the courtyard. The room was dark and looked to be empty.

For some reason, I wanted to see that man again, see him there, even if he was fucking another woman. I didn't understand this strange thinking though, this pull he had on me. I shook my head and grabbed my raincoat and purse. In my rush to get out of the café last night, I'd forgotten to pay the bill. I'd drop by this morning and take care of that.

One my way out, I pulled the hood of my raincoat up over my head and opened my dingy umbrella. I needed to get a new one. For now though, I jumped over puddles and quickly walked toward the café, remembering the events of last night, seeing the stranger's blue, blue eyes, the look in them burned into my brain. I wasn't sure why I couldn't stop thinking about him. Surely, they would check out of the hotel soon and I'd likely never see him again.

Which would be a good thing, right?

The café was already busy with most patrons standing at the bar, drinking their cappuccinos. It was cheaper than getting a table to drink your coffee at the bar, so many locals did it. I scanned the room in the guise of looking for the waiter who had served me last night, but some part of me was almost hoping to see *him* here. But that was silly.

I found the waiter and walked toward him as he cleared a table. "Um, hello, I was here last night."

He recognized me and smiled. "Yes, hello," he said, continuing with his work.

At least he wasn't mad.

"I forgot to pay. I was in a rush and only realized it when I got home. I'm really sorry, I hope I can..."

"No, it's okay. Your friend took care of the check." He moved toward the bar to unload his tray and pick up the next order.

"My friend?" My heart began to race.

"Yes, the man. Tall, dark suit. He came as soon as you left."

Could it be *him*? *The* man? But why?

"He paid for me?"

"Yes."

"Are you sure? I don't really know him."

"Yes, I am sure. Please, it's very busy."

I nodded. "Okay, yes, I'm sorry."

I slipped my wallet back into my purse and went to the bar to order an espresso, baffled. Had he followed me to the café last night after all? I had hoped he wouldn't have had a good look at me through that window, but I'd been so caught up that I couldn't be sure how long he'd been watching me while I'd been watching them.

Again, I flushed with shame at my behavior.

Quickly drinking my espresso, I put two Euros down on the counter before I forgot again. But just as I turned to go, the news cut into the program that was showing on the small TV behind the bar. Although I couldn't understand all they said, I did recognize the photograph of the woman plastered on the screen, behind which was the scene of a crime.

I turned back around to watch.

The reporter spoke too fast and my Italian was so very limited. They stated the woman's name. It sounded like she was an American. They then cut to the scene where an ambulance waited with its lights flashing and reporters surrounded the gathered police.

Two men rolled a gurney toward the waiting vehicle. My throat grew tight at what lay on top of it: a body covered over completely by a blanket, long blonde hair blowing in the wet, rainy morning.

For a moment, I entertained the thought that maybe they'd covered her to give her privacy. Maybe it wasn't what I was thinking. But when they loaded the gurney onto the ambulance, her arm slipped out from beneath the sheet that covered her.

The dried blood made my stomach heave and I turned

quickly to the door, forgetting my umbrella in my haste to exit the café. I all but ran through the rain back to the hotel, trying to process what I had just seen.

Murdered. The woman I'd been watching through the window at the hotel had been murdered.

I remembered what I had thought when I'd seen the man, first in that hotel room, then at the bar. Danger. A clear warning had gone up for me. Was it possible he'd done this to the woman? But why?

No, I couldn't think of this. It was unreal — this kind of stuff only happened in the movies. And besides, maybe I'd been wrong? I'd never really gotten a good look at her face and when I had, she'd had a cock stuffed in her mouth the one time, and the others, her face had been contorted either from pleasure or pain. I still didn't know which.

I remembered reading somewhere that one's expression in intense pleasure or pain is hard to distinguish. Why I thought of that in this moment, I had no idea. Besides, I hadn't really been paying attention to her. I'd been entirely too engrossed in watching him, watching his face, his body, his hips as he'd fucked her, his eyes as he'd come.

The memory made me wet even now, even after what I'd just seen on TV. I stopped at a convenience store and bought a new umbrella, forcing myself to slow down and breathe as I did. I was being ridiculous. I was on edge, that was all. After my conversation with Allison and then seeing the news, my mind was making things up.

I was safe. Jason didn't know where I was, and as horrible as the woman's murder was, I'd been mistaken. The woman who had been killed wasn't anyone I knew.

I opened my new umbrella and walked back to my apartment. Ever since I'd told the detectives what Jason had done, I'd been on the run. It was as if I'd become trained to constantly look over my shoulder, to tense at every little noise.

I had to stop this. Yes, he was out of prison, but he wouldn't find me. I had changed my name and I'd moved so many times in the last couple of years *I* could barely keep track of where I'd been. There was no way he could track me. I wasn't even in the US anymore. I had to try to relax, start to live again.

It was easier said than done though. I knew Jason would keep searching for me. When he'd been released early, I even considered not going back to sign the paperwork and claim the money. *That* was how afraid I was of him.

But it was money my sister had left for me, and I had thirty days after my birthday to pick it up before it reverted to Jason and Allison. It was the way the will had been written. Probably something my stepfather had done, considering he'd have to have been the one to have given her the money.

I used the word inheritance now, but in truth, it was money to shut us up. To shut my sister and me up about what had happened.

But I hadn't shut-up. I'd sent Jason to prison. He was supposed to serve fifteen years, but he had gotten out early, and now, he wanted revenge.

Closing my umbrella, I entered the lobby of the hotel, noticing right away the two police officers standing at the front desk talking to an employee. Dread filled my belly. What if I'd been right? What if it was the woman from across my room that had been murdered? And what if the murderer was the man I could identify?

"Key for room 412," I said.

The young man nodded and retrieved the key to my room. They had those old-fashioned keys you'd leave at the desk on your way out. Modern security measures hadn't yet reached this hotel. It would have been charming if it wasn't frightening.

"What's happening?" I asked the agent after taking my key.

He glanced over at the police and the manager. "A woman's body was found a few blocks away early this morning. She was a guest of our hotel."

I shivered at his words, my hands suddenly clammy and cold. "Oh."

"Terrible," he said, shaking his head.

"I saw the news."

"I can assure you the hotel is secure. The attack did not take place here."

I didn't know what else to say and glanced once more at the police before walking toward the stairs. If they questioned me, considering the position of my room to the dead woman's room, I would have to lie. I couldn't take a chance on being found, on my true identity being revealed. Jason would be here before I could sneeze. No, I had to get out of here and I had to think of a way to go back to claim the money without being found out.

The hallway was quiet when I reached my floor. I kept my gaze down as I made my way to my room, noting again the splotches on the old, dark red carpet. I wondered if the police would be up in her room now. Actually, I knew they would be..

Reaching my door, I first listened. I had learned to do that over the last years, to pay closer attention, to watch people around me. To always be aware and to know the fastest way to the exit.

All was quiet though and I slid my key into the lock, turning it simultaneously with the doorknob to open the door. Although it was daytime, I'd kept the heavy curtains drawn and between that and the rainy, overcast day, the room was dark.

I closed the door behind me and set the key, my purse, and the umbrella down, my gaze on the window. I went to it slowly and just drew the curtains far enough apart that I could see out but not be seen myself.

The room across the courtyard looked very different from mine. The lights were on and even brighter lighting had been brought in.

Two uniformed officers along with several figures in civilian clothing worked, gathering evidence, trying to put together the puzzle of a murder.

There was a sudden, bright flash then and I gasped, dropping the curtain and pressing my back against the wall, my hand to my heart. I forced myself to take a deep breath and calm down. Of course, they were taking photographs of the scene. And if they were smart, they'd question the guest from across the courtyard whose room looked directly into the dead woman's room.

I reached a trembling hand out to switch on the dimmest lamp. It took a little feeling around to find the cord and I pulled on it, but the exact moment I did was the exact moment I saw him.

I let out a little scream and jumped backward, pressing my back to the wall as he rose to his feet and put a finger to his lips.

"Shh."

How had I not seen him? How had I not sensed him? He hadn't even been hiding, he'd been sitting there on the couch waiting for me.

I swallowed as he stopped just a few inches from me. I turned my gaze up to his, his cold, blue eyes piercing through me as his gaze bore into mine before scanning me from head to toe.

I don't know how I didn't scream then. Don't know how I stood there, trembling as I was, and it was only when he reached a hand to my chin and lifted my face to his that I even remembered to breathe.

"You like to watch, Mia?" he asked, his voice a low, deep rumble that made every hair on my body stand on end, brought every nerve ending to life.

I would have screamed then.

I opened my mouth to just as he clamped his large, gloved hand over it, pushing me against the wall, stifling my scream. Inhaling leather, I wrapped my hands around his forearm, my limbs acting purely out of instinct. I knew in that instant that all my fears were true. That this man, this man whom I'd watched fuck the dead woman, this man who had aroused me more than any other, who'd had me shame-fully watching so intimate an act, was a killer. I knew it as surely as I knew my own name.

It was then I realized that he'd *said* my name. I would have asked how he knew it, how he'd gotten into my room, but at that moment, terror held me paralyzed in its grip.

"Now, are you going to scream if I take my hand away?"

I tried to shake my head no but he was pressing so hard that I couldn't move it. Was he here to kill me, knowing I'd seen his face? That I was a potential witness who could identify him?

I tried to say that I wouldn't scream but it came out muffled against his palm. He took a moment to peek between the curtains at the room across the way before returning his attention to me, his gaze moving to my hands, which gripped his forearm.

"There's a reason you haven't gone to the police yet," he said. "I'm incredibly curious what that reason is."

I tugged on his arm but he only pressed harder.

"Put your hands behind your back and keep them there," he said. "Do it and I'll release you. Scream and I'll fuck you up, understand?"

I nodded and slowly let go of his forearm to clasp my hands behind my back.

"Good girl," he said, his hand still over my mouth, his gaze traveling down to my chest where my raincoat had fallen open to reveal the simple white blouse I'd worn underneath.

The material was a fine cotton and I followed his gaze to where my nipple pushed through the lace of my bra against the too-thin fabric.

Casually, he brought the knuckles of one hand to that breast and brushed them over the nipple. I sucked in a breath.

He gave me a knowing look, and, without thinking, I grabbed for his forearm again, holding it with all the strength I could muster, warning him not to touch me even though it wasn't repulsion I felt. It was quite the opposite, in fact.

He simply grinned, one corner of his mouth curling upward.

"So you can watch me fuck, but I can't even touch this pretty little nipple?" he asked, somehow moving his arm so that he now gripped my wrists and pressed them against the wall over my head.

He looked at me for a moment while I struggled against his hold, then, with eyes locked on mine, lowered his head to that nipple and closed his mouth around it, moaning as if he were tasting the most delicious thing imaginable.

I stared, catching my breath as he sucked, his breath hot, his mouth wet. Without any conscious thought, the sensation sent a signal directly to my clit. But when he closed his teeth over the nipple and bit just hard enough, I cried out into his palm, squeezing my eyes shut.

He straightened then, looking down at the place his mouth had just been, at the wet spot he'd left on my blouse.

"Very pretty," he said. "I can't wait to see how the rest of you tastes."

Panic struck, but just as my mind processed what he'd said, there was a sound just outside the door. Two men talking.

"What the fuck?" the man who held me said. But he didn't get much more out before we heard the sound of a bullet fired through the silencer of a gun. I would have screamed, but the intruder grabbed me and pulled me to the other side of the bed, pushing me down onto the floor and reaching into his coat pocket to retrieve his own pistol.

Wood splintered as they busted the door open and the man beside me shoved me under the bed. I knew instinctively to keep quiet. I watched from where I was as two men in suits walked into my room. I had to clamp my hand over my own mouth to keep quiet, tears of panic filling my eyes. These were Jason's men. I knew it. How could this be happening?

The men split up and when one approached the bed, the one who'd been waiting for me in my room moved, his weapon ready, a shot fired at close enough range that it was silenced not only by the silencer on the weapon itself but also by the man's body. A second bullet was fired and this time I did scream as I saw one of the intruders fall to the floor, his eyes still open, his gun just falling out of his hand.

There was commotion as another shot rang out amid

sounds of a struggle and I knew I had to act. As scared as I was, I dragged myself over the dusty floor under the bed and reached for the fallen man's pistol just as another body landed with a thud. Before I could think, a hand clamped around my ankle and dragged me roughly out from under the bed, a loose spring tearing my coat and scraping my shoulder as I went, a small scream leaving my lips.

I didn't even have a chance to use my weapon — not that I really knew how — because as soon as he saw it, he gripped my wrist and roughly brought it down on the hardwood floor, making me to cry out again at the pain, my weapon clattering to the floor.

He pocketed it as he hauled me to my feet and dragged me by the arm to pick up the second weapon. He turned to me for an instant, his eyes fiery as he held his gun at my jaw.

"I don't know who the hell those two were, but I just saved your life. Fucking keep quiet or I'll end it. Understand?"

I nodded fast, tears blurring my vision.

He dragged me to the door, grabbing my purse on the way and tucking the hand that held the pistol into his coat pocket. He walked me down the corridor and toward the side exit, which I knew would trigger an alarm if we opened the door. I hoped at least that if the alarm went off, the police would hear.

I knew I couldn't let this man take me. I had to get away from him somehow.

We walked quickly through the door that led to the back stairwell and just as it closed behind us, I heard the sound of men running. I couldn't see them but I knew they were the police. My captor held on to my purse and dragged me down the stairs with him, righting me when I stumbled, but not once stopping or slowing down, not easing his grip on my arm. He was focused, his gaze hard, unreadable, and when we reached the exit, I realized I was out of luck.

The alarmed door was propped open by a brick so that all my captor had to do was push it wide enough for us to exit.

Rain still fell in sheets and we ran toward a waiting vehicle parked at the end of the alley. Opening the driver's side door, he shoved me inside, forcing me over the gearshift and the parking brake, never once releasing his hold on me until he slapped a handcuff over my wrist and secured me to the door.

I watched him, his features tense as he started the car and drove into traffic with the confidence of a local, weaving through cars and driving out of the city and toward the highway.

5

JULIEN

"*M*ind telling me who the fuck those men were, Mia?" I asked once we'd merged onto the highway and were well on our way out of the city.

"How do you know my name?"

I glanced at her, her voice sweet, making her seem younger, the slight tremble of it giving away her fear. I pulled her passport out of my pocket, noting the way her expression changed, then tucked it back into my coat. "Why were two men at your apartment with guns?"

"Why were you?"

I grinned at that. "Do you remember what got the kitten killed, Kitten?"

Her eyes went wide and I had to laugh.

"It's cat. It's what got the cat killed," she corrected, her voice a whisper.

I touched her face, then patted her cheek twice and kept my hand there. "Well, I like kitten better. I think it fits." She jerked her head away, and when she did, I gripped her chin and made her look at me, wiping any hint of joking from my expression. I wasn't playing a game and she needed to know that. "Tell me what killed the kitten." When she didn't answer right away, I squeezed a little, making her flinch.

"Curiosity."

"Good girl." I let her go and turned my attention back to the road.

"Did you kill her?" she asked.

"I think there's a much more important question you should be asking right now, don't you?"

She wiped at a few of her tears with her free hand but kept looking at me. What I saw in her eyes, wasn't just fear. There was something else there, something more, a darkness, an edge. She was a survivor, like me.

"Are you going to kill me?"

"Clever kitten. Well, I can't leave witnesses behind. It's not the mark of a good killer, is it?"

"I won't tell, I promise. I had the chance and I didn't say anything."

"I know and I find that increasingly curious. Especially after your friends showed up."

"They're not friends." She turned away, her expression closed off.

"Who were they then?"

"If I tell you, will you let me go?"

"Probably not, no."

"Did you do it?"

"Do what?" I asked, knowing all along what she was asking. She knew the answer, but she needed for me to say it. I exited one highway and merged onto another, taking a toll ticket.

Fucking Italy. Still used paper tickets to collect tolls.

"Kill her. Did you kill your girlfriend?"

The fact that she thought the blonde had been my girlfriend surprised me. "She wasn't my girlfriend, but yes, I did kill her."

"Oh my God," she started, trying to pull on her cuffed arm. "Oh God…"

"Relax, Mia. If I wanted you dead, you'd be dead by now, don't you think?"

"Then why aren't I?"

"Because I'm curious why there was a hit on you."

She clammed up again and wouldn't look at me when she did answer. "I don't know what you're talking about."

"Not only a peeping Tom, but a liar as well. And a bad one at that."

"What are you going to do to me?"

"That depends."

"Can I at least know your name?"

I looked at her, her question catching me off guard for some reason.

"Julien." When was the last time I'd told someone my real name? I couldn't remember.

She nodded, as if trying to fit the name to the man, but before she could ask anything else, my phone rang. I reached into my pocket and checked the display. It was Ryan.

"That was reasonably fast," I said.

"How'd you run into this one?" Ryan asked.

That did not sound good. "Why?"

"What's the name she's going by? Mia Andrews?"

Fuck.

This wasn't good. "An alias?"

"Yep. I'll need fingerprints to verify, but Mia St. Rose disappeared a couple of years ago."

"Disappeared from where?"

"Philadelphia. Ring a bell, yet?"

I glanced over at Mia who now watched me.

"Why don't you fill me in," I asked, my eyes remaining on her.

"Samuel and Jason St. Rose. Remember them? Samuel, the father, was under investigation for money laundering for some pretty bad people, including the Casanov family. Investigation is stalled — I'll have to look further into that. But Jason is supposed to be serving his fifteen years."

I didn't know much about those pieces of shit, but I knew about the Casanov family.

"Go on." It was all coming together.

"Your girl's stepbrother was released early for good behavior a few weeks ago."

Fucking system. Assholes with money could still manipulate it. But assholes like Samuel and Jason St. Rose were exactly why I had a job.

"And?" I didn't care about the St. Roses. I wanted to know about the girl.

"Stepsister's testimony had put him away."

"What did he allegedly do?"

"Files are sealed. She was a minor at the time of the crime. Want my guess?"

The look in Mia's eyes when I glanced her way was one of panic, of fear, but in the depths of her gaze, there was something else I saw, something I now recognized as shame.

"No," I said to Ryan. I could imagine what he'd done to her, but I did not need that confirmation. I couldn't afford to know.

"Well, there's money on her head." Ryan paused a moment. "Ah, here's why the investigation stalled out. Turns out there's a book missing. The ledger from the senior St. Rose's business. I can only imagine what kind of information is in there. And, even more interesting, Jason St. Rose wants her back. Bad."

"How bad?"

"Quarter of a million dollars bad."

"Quarter of a million, huh?" I repeated, glancing at my captive again. "And you're sure it's the kid who marked her, not the father?"

"Not a doubt. Send me something with her prints on them and I'll confirm if it's her or not. And if it is her, we have a deal, right?"

The deal was that I paid Ryan ten percent. It bought trust, and had made Ryan a wealthy man. Just as killing had made me a wealthy man.

"Deal stands. Just make sure you keep your mouth shut on this one."

"I'm offended you have to say that at all." There was a feigned note of upset in Ryan's voice that he couldn't quite pull off. "I thought we were friends."

Friends. That was a joke. I didn't have friends.

"Shut the fuck up. I'll send you something tomorrow."

I hung up and turned to her. "Looks like I won't be killing you after all."

She opened her mouth to ask a question, then closed it again.

"Turns out your brother sent those men. You've got a quarter of a million dollar bounty on your head. Why is he so anxious to get you back, Mia?"

She stared, all the color draining from her face. She was more afraid of him than she was of me. Considering she knew what I'd just done, that baffled me.

"He's not my brother," she started, shifting her gaze out the side window. "*Stepbrother*. And if you take me to him, I'm dead."

6

MIA

I watched Julien as he drove, but images of him in that hotel room interrupted. His large hands gripped the steering wheel and his expression was serious, his gaze focused on the road ahead.

Sitting this close to him, I picked up the subtle scent of aftershave, and more that that. He took up so much space, too much. It was as if he were more real now, more so than when he'd been in that other room separated from me.

I'd known he was attractive, but this close up, seeing the chiseled bones of his face, the set of his jaw, he looked almost elegant. Not like he'd looked in that room. Not while he'd been...

He chose that moment to glance my way and I knew I had just turned bright red when I felt the heat of embarrassment spreading across my face.

"What?" he asked.

I shook my head. Looks were deceiving. I had to remember that this man was a killer. "Nothing. Where are you taking me?"

He checked his watch. "We'll drive a few more hours

then get a hotel for the night where you can tell me the bedtime story of your life."

I wouldn't be telling him any stories. He'd be disappointed if he believed that I would. But a hotel was good. At a hotel, there would be people. And if there were people, there was a chance I could escape.

My purse, which contained my wallet and some money, was in the backseat, and he had my passport in his pocket. I'd just have to figure out a way to grab that before I ran.

Julien reached to turn on the radio and sat back to drive, his attention fully on the road now.

I studied him, his face in profile. His dark hair was clean-cut and his skin had an olive tone. His jaw was covered in scruff spotted with gray and the set of his mouth was hard, although his lips were quite full and sensual. He actually fit with the Italians in looks, except for his eyes. They were a bright, icy blue. I bet he fooled a lot of women with those eyes, but I'd seen what hid in their depths. I'd seen it when I'd been watching him. I'd seen a cruelty in them, a darkness.

And I couldn't explain why that darkness drew me even as it repelled me, scared me to death. The man was a murderer.

"Why did you kill her?"

He glanced at me, his eyes scanning my face before he answered. His answer was plain.

"I was hired to. She was my mark." He watched me, his expression neutral. "And you're a witness who can identify me. Can you guess what that means for you?"

When I didn't speak, he continued.

"Remember something, Mia St. Rose. When you ask a question, you should be ready to hear the answer."

I hadn't been ready to hear that.

His words left me shivering. They were so cold, the way he spoke them chilling. And when he said it, his eyes went flat, as if this were a casual, meaningless conversation. As if someone hadn't been killed.

I dropped my gaze first, unable to hold his. The man frightened me, deeply.

When I'd first seen him and the woman in the hotel room across from mine a few nights ago, it had been by accident. I'd pulled the curtains open merely with the intention of opening the window. I'd just wanted to get some fresh air.

But when I'd seen what I'd seen, this beautiful man naked, a woman kneeling before him, sucking him off, his grip on her hair hard, his gaze on the top of her head as he pulled her head back and forth, I couldn't look away. I just couldn't. The act was beautiful and base, all at once.

He was cruel and she seemed to worship at his feet.

When he'd finished, he'd come on her face. I remembered that, I remembered feeling both offended and madly aroused by the humiliating act. That and the fact that he'd made her remain like that, on her knees, her hands clasped at the back of her head while the cum dried on her face.

He'd gone to have a shower and when he'd emerged fresh and clean, he'd dressed while watching her, not once saying a word, and then he'd left. I'd watched the woman after he'd gone. I'd seen her remain as he'd left her for the next half hour before finally climbing to her feet to clean herself up. What sort of man wielded power like that over a woman?

A man like him, like my captor.

"You reliving those nights?" he asked, grinning.

"What? No!" I lied, mortified. Was I so obvious?

He pulled off toward the exit, slowing down, reaching

into the back seat to grab a sweater and toss it over my lap to hide the handcuffs.

"One word and the old woman's dead. Clear?" He opened his jacket to let me see the gun.

I nodded.

Julien handed over the ticket, spoke a few words in fluent Italian with the woman at the toll, paid, and drove off. He'd actually smiled when talking to her. Would he truly have killed her if I'd alerted her? What kind of person could do that?

"Almost there," he said to me. "You hungry?"

I hadn't eaten all day and we'd been driving for several hours. "Yes."

He nodded and drove a little farther until we came upon a roadside restaurant. There were three other cars in the parking lot and once we'd parked, he turned to me.

"I could stretch my legs and eat something. If you're going to do anything stupid, I'd suggest you save it for the hotel so no one but you gets hurt, understood?"

"Why are you doing this?"

He feigned confusion for a moment. "Money, of course. Why else? But it's better than being dead, isn't it? You should thank your brother when I get you back to him. He saved your life."

I swallowed, watching his face for any signs of humanity, and finding none.

"There are kids in there. Are we clear on behavior, Mia?"

I nodded and he climbed out of the car. He came around to get me, releasing me from the handcuffs and hauling me out.

He kept me close as we walked inside, his fingers digging into my arm. He chose a booth at the very back of the place and pushed me in to sit, removing his jacket, leaving him in only a t-shirt and jeans, before sliding in next to me. I scooted away, but he came closer so that our arms touched, his bare skin reminding me of the art that decorated his body, the tattoos that covered most of his chest, both arms and one part of his back. I looked at the one on his forearm more closely. It was a date some fifteen years ago.

"What's that?" I couldn't help but ask.

He looked at it, and emotion passed through his eyes, something sad at first which then morphed into something else, something akin to hate.

"The day I became what I am," he said, his gaze on mine.

I knew to tread carefully and I remembered his words from the last time I'd asked a question:

When you ask a question, you should be ready to hear the answer.

I wasn't ready to hear this answer.

A waitress stopped at our table, looking at me for a moment before turning her full attention to him. The way she pushed her hip out and smiled, I knew she found him attractive. He knew it too, because he actually flirted with her.

I didn't speak Italian half as well as he did, but I'd been here long enough to understand some of it, and even if I couldn't understand a word, the tone of his voice and the look on his face would have told me he was flirting right back.

"I ordered for you," he said, handing the menus back. He had a smile for her, but only a cold look for me.

I thought about telling him I could have ordered for myself, but I didn't care what I ate. I was thinking of how I could make my escape but knew it would be ridiculous for me to try just yet. He had the car keys and my passport and I knew he meant it when he said people would get hurt. I'd have to wait until tonight.

"Tell me why your brother has put a price on your head," he said.

"*Stepbrother*. Because I testified against him and put him behind bars. Temporarily, at least."

Which threw a kink into my plans. Jason wanted me more than he wanted that million. I was smart enough to know he'd have men watching the law office and wouldn't be surprised if the attorney was in his pocket too. His and Samuel's.

"So, he wants revenge."

"He'll kill me if you take me to him. You have to know that. He's... like you."

That made him pause. "Like me how?" he asked, grinning.

The waitress returned with plates of hot sandwiches and I tried to formulate my response in those moments she was with us. I didn't want to piss him off, but he didn't seem volatile. In fact, he was eerily composed, considering what he had done that morning.

I picked up my sandwich and took a bite, avoiding his gaze.

"Tell me, Mia. I'm curious."

"Are you American? You speak Italian fluently, and you look Italian, but you also sound like an American."

"Does it matter?"

Well, I guess it didn't. I shook my head.

"Now, tell me."

I glanced at him from the corner of my eye.

He smiled and leaned in close. "Don't worry, whatever you say, I won't kill you. You're worth a quarter of a million dollars to me."

Then he winked before opening his mouth to expose a row of perfect white teeth — well, perfect except for the canines which seemed a little too sharp — and bit into his sandwich.

"He's a mercenary. Just like you," I said, putting my sandwich down. I'd lost my appetite.

He paused, actually seeming surprised for a moment.

It was my turn to smile. "Don't ask a question for which you're not prepared to hear the answer, Julien."

7

JULIEN

*T*he rest of our lunch was quiet. She'd rattled me. I didn't even know why though, because she hadn't told me anything I didn't already know. I waited for her to climb into the passenger seat and re-cuffed her. I then slammed the door shut and walked around the back of the vehicle.

The last of the sun disappeared and the streetlights farther down began to turn on. The one over our car flickered twice, but remained dark.

Good.

Dark fit my mood.

She'd used my own words against me, and for some reason, I didn't like her saying my name. Why I'd told it to her in the first place baffled me. I'd been taken by surprise when she'd asked. I guess I never thought anyone would give enough of a fuck to ask.

She doesn't give a fuck, asshole.

Standing at the back of the car, I took a cigarette out of my pocket and lit it, all while watching the back of her head. She was pretty. Not really my type, but pretty. I liked them a little dirtier, like the waitress. Taking a long drag on the cigarette, I turned to lean against the trunk. I was on edge. It was the killing. I needed to blow off steam, that was all.

As if on cue, the waitress who'd served us walked out of the back of the restaurant. She glanced toward me, maybe surprised to see another car on this side of the building. Customers usually parked out front.

I smiled and tossed my cigarette to the ground before walking over to her.

She glanced at Mia who sat watching us from inside the car, then leaned her hip against the hood of her car and waited.

I didn't look back at Mia when I went to the woman, and she seemed to know exactly why I was coming. But when I got close enough for her to see my face, my eyes, her smile disappeared, a momentary panic replacing the flirtation that had brightened her face a minute ago.

Well, that was what I did to women. I scared them.

But I also fucked them and made them come. Being scared only made them wetter for it.

Taking her by the arms, I kissed her roughly, mashing my lips against hers. She tasted bitter, used, but I didn't care. I only needed one thing.

Turning her around, I bent her over the hood and reached into my pocket for a condom, glancing toward my vehicle as I pushed the girl's jeans and panties down over her hips and to her knees. I saw Mia's face, her eyes wide as she watched. I turned back to the girl, rubbing her back, pushing her shirt up as I did, looking at her full, round ass.

I didn't waste words, but remained silent while unzipping my jeans and rolling the condom over my cock. I then gripped her hips and pulled her ass cheeks apart with my thumbs, finding her little cunt shaved bare and already glistening.

But it wasn't her I looked at when I shoved my cock inside her pussy. It was Mia.

I watched her just like I had those other times.

I saw her face, saw her expression change as I thrust into the whore's cunt, and waited for Mia to meet my gaze.

When she did, I smiled, narrowing my eyes, pressing my fingers into the girl's flesh as I fucked her, again thinking of Mia, seeing her pretty eyes on me, imagining her on her knees before me, taking my cock into her mouth, imagining her on her back, her legs wide, her pussy open for me to fuck.

I groaned, pressing against the girl's fleshy bottom as I came, barely hearing the sounds she made, and when I was done, I slid out of her, pulling the condom off and tossing it into the bushes. Turning the girl around, I pushed her to her knees.

"Clean it," I said.

She looked surprised for a moment, but then opened her greedy little mouth and licked my cock clean. If I'd allowed myself to, I'd have gotten hard again, but I didn't want that. I wanted to see Mia's face. I wanted to get back to my car and get to a hotel and have a good look at her, at all of her. Hell, she'd watched me fuck. It was my turn to watch.

Buttoning my jeans, I went back to my car and got in.

Mia turned her still shocked face away from me and cleared her throat. I didn't smile, didn't feel like I'd won anything. I had expected to though.

I knew she'd be shocked and that was what I wanted. I was a man who took, that was all. I never gave, and when the time came, I'd take from her too.

Driving out of the parking lot, I switched on the radio. I needed the noise. It masked the tension in the car.

So, her stepbrother was looking for her because she'd put him in jail. I wanted to know more. I'd call Ryan for more specifics but I'd hear her story tonight. I'd make her tell it to me naked while I looked over every inch of her. My cock stirred at the thought and I glanced at my captive who remained looking out the window, her eyes still wide, and turned my own gaze to the road, trying to ignore this strange feeling of guilt.

Guilt? No, it couldn't be that. To feel guilt, one had to feel something else. Regret for one. But worse than that, I didn't care what Mia St. Rose thought of me. I didn't care if I offended or shocked her.

Why the hell are you even entertaining those thoughts?

I turned up the volume on the radio and we drove without speaking for another hour until finally, Mia broke the silence.

"Why did you do that?"

I looked at her, met her defiant gaze, the green color like a blazing emerald. There was fire within those eyes, the fire of a survivor, of strength.

"Why did I fuck her?"

I saw it took some doing for her to keep her eyes on me. I liked it, liked seeing her struggle. She nodded once, her forehead creased, the expression on her face almost one of anger.

"Blow off steam," I said, looking at the road again. It seemed I could only take her direct gaze in small increments and that bothered me. It was weak.

"So, you *fuck* strangers to blow off steam?"

I smiled. "So, you *watch* strangers *fuck* to blow off steam?"

She glared.

"What? Would you rather I fuck you?"

"Screw you, asshole."

I veered so fast to the side of the road that she let out a small scream and grabbed hold of the dashboard with her free hand. Hitting the brakes hard, I grabbed a handful of her thick, dark hair and tugged her head backwards. She gasped, her frightened eyes wide.

"Listen to me, girl. I hold your life in my hands. You live at my pleasure, understand?"

"Let me go, you prick!"

I tugged harder until tears filled her eyes and she gripped my arm with her free hand.

"I may be a prick, but at least I don't hide from what I am. You? You hide behind a curtain and watch. And I bet if I were to slide a hand inside those tight jeans of yours, I'd find your cunt wet from what I just allowed you to witness."

She yelped, trying to push back against the seat as far as possible as I ran my hand down over her belly and toward her crotch. Keeping my eyes on hers, I undid the button and took the zipper down.

"Please don't."

"Please don't, what?" I asked, fingers brushing over the white lace of her panties. I'd have to get a better look at those later.

She mewled when I pushed two fingers down until I felt the little patch of hair.

"I'm sorry, Julien. I'm sorry."

She said it again. She said my fucking name and it made me stop. I looked at her, at the terror in her reddened eyes. I wasn't a fucking rapist and she was looking at me like I was.

I released her, more bothered by that look than I cared to consider.

"Just be quiet."

She sniffled, looking at her lap, trembling fingers of one hand trying to work her jeans closed. I pulled back onto the road, my mind back on what I was supposed to be doing, on where I was going.

"I'm half Italian, half American. I was born in Italy to an Italian mother and an American father," I said, surprising myself, surprising her. From the corner of my eye I watched her turn toward me, but I kept my gaze on the road. "I spent the first six years of my life here. After that, we moved to the US and spent summers back here. Then they died and I was handed over to the American foster care system."

Until my grandmother was sober enough to take custody of us, anyway. That had been the plan. The hope. But hope made you a beggar. It was a waste of fucking time.

I accelerated, feeling her eyes bore into me, burning into the side of my head. I didn't need her pity. That wasn't why I was telling her the story. Actually, I hadn't a fucking clue why I *was* telling her.

The foster care system sucked. Our family home here in Italy, which had been in my mother's family for generations, had been passed down to my brother and myself. But since it was just me now, it belonged wholly to me.

I didn't come back here often. Too many memories, and memories were time's way of fucking with you. At least fucking with me.

I'd paid to keep up the house for years, even though it sat empty most of the time. Now, it looked like I'd have need for the place for the first time in, well, a long time.

I'd never brought anyone here before and didn't want to think about why I was bringing her now, but that was what I was doing. The village was a few hours away though, and at that moment, I was too tired to think about the whys any further.

I drove for another hour before pulling into the parking lot of a roadside hotel. I killed the ignition and turned to Mia who looked at me with a little more caution since our previous little roadside chat.

Good. She needs to be afraid.

"We're walking inside and getting a room for the night. Are you going to be good?" I touched my hand to the pocket that held my pistol.

"Are you going to hurt me?"

I studied her, wondering if she realized the depth of her question. At least its depth to me. "Probably."

Her face began to crumple, the stress of the past twenty-four hours finally catching up with her. I enjoyed tears, just not this kind.

Sighing, I took her face in my hand and made her look at me. "I'm not going to rape you, if that's what you're thinking." I wasn't. She just didn't know yet how easily she'd give it up to me when it came time for me to take it. "Okay?"

"Not okay," she said, sniffling and wiping away the last of her tears as she jerked her face out of my grasp. "But I don't have much choice right now, do I?"

The girl intrigued me. She was afraid of me, knew what I was capable of, yet she confronted me. She didn't tuck her tail between her legs and bow her head, as I expected her to.

"No, you don't, Mia. Be good."

8

MIA

*J*ulien checked us into the hotel while I stood quietly at his side. The clerk at the desk was a teenage girl who had her nose in a book until we showed up. Obviously, not a place that saw a lot of action.

I thought about what he'd told me in the car, what he'd said about his family. When I'd asked him earlier where he was from and he hadn't answered, I figured that was it. I wondered what had made him tell me, and, more importantly, I had a feeling he was asking himself the same thing.

I tried to figure out where he was taking me. We were headed toward the mountains and I just figured he'd have taken us straight to an airport to get me back to Philadelphia as soon as possible in order to hand me over to my step-brother to collect the money.

I thought about telling him about the million. While he filled out the check-in form, I questioned whether or not it would help me to do that. He would turn me in for a quarter of a million dollars but he'd also be taking a chance that

Jason wouldn't pay him at all. Jason would just as easily kill him, in my opinion.

I made a note to mention that, although it would have surprised me if the thought hadn't crossed his mind already. Julien was a professional killer. I had a feeling he'd be able to handle my stepbrother.

My other option, the one aside from escape, was to tell him about the million. Maybe if I offered to pay him half, he'd help me get it. If there was one thing I knew, it was that Julien could, if he wanted to, keep me safe. If there was half a million in it for him, would he do that? But then, what would stop him from just taking all of it?

Well, it wasn't like it was being handed over in a big bag of unmarked bills. That latter worry wasn't one at all. I'd transfer the funds to his account once I got the million and then I'd disappear again. This time for good.

Although it would be a hell of a lot easier to disappear with a full million dollars than half.

"Ready, honey?" Julien gave me a mocking grin, holding the key up in front of my face. "Got us a king size bed."

I simply glared at him, and somehow, it managed to wipe that grin off his face as he steered me toward the elevators.

Our room was on the ninth floor and the elevator crept along, the doors opening at every floor along the way for some reason.

"Think it's haunted?" Julien asked.

If he was trying to be silly or casual, it wasn't working. I saw his hand slide into his coat the first time it happened, ready to pull out his pistol if he had to.

"I guess you have to walk around with your hand over your gun all the time, given the type of work you're in." I looked straight ahead, watching the doors slide closed on the eighth floor with a now familiar squeak.

Note to self: take the stairs if you can manage to get out of here.

"I'm cautious, that's certain - - but no more than you. Difference is, I'm better at it than you are."

I gave him a sideways glance as the doors opened once more, and Julien led us out into the corridor and to our room, which was just a few doors down.

Once there, he let us inside and switched on the light. It was a standard room in a cheap hotel: one king size bed, a TV, nightstands on either side of the bed, and a bathroom.

"I bet the police are looking for me," I said, going to the window and looking out over the highway at the lights of passing cars.

"I'd say so, but I think you'll do what you can not to be found."

I drew the curtains closed and turned to him. He was right. I did not want the police to find me. I didn't want anyone to find me. I wanted to disappear. I needed to disappear.

"Have you considered the fact that Jason may not pay you once you deliver me? I mean, what's to stop him from killing you?"

"I can take care of myself," he said easily, folding his coat over the back of a chair, tucking the revolver into his jeans and setting his wallet, the handcuffs and a few coins onto the chipped wood of the TV stand. "You want to have a shower?"

I nodded.

"All right. I'll let you go first," he said. "Undress."

"I'll undress in the bathroom."

"I'd rather you did it in front of me so I can be sure you're not carrying any sort of weapons."

"I'm not carrying weapons," I said, folding my arms across my chest in an effort to remain casual, or at least to appear so.

"Well, I'd just prefer to be sure," he said, grinning again and leaning against the wall. "If you want to have a shower, you'll get undressed now. Otherwise"—he picked up the handcuffs and held them up for me to see—"I'll get you cuffed and have one myself. Of course, I'll have to strip you anyway, but you'd probably prefer doing it yourself. Besides, you've seen me naked and you've watched me fuck — more than once — and I haven't so much as seen a little tittie."

My mouth dropped open.

"What's it going to be?" he asked, taking a step toward me.

"I hate you," I said, reaching to slide my raincoat off my shoulders.

He shrugged a shoulder. "If I gave a fuck, that would matter. Besides, I don't actually think you hate me." He walked toward me with that grin on his face, the one that said he knew me better than I knew myself.

I took a step back, my fingers frozen on the button I was undoing at the top of my blouse.

"I think, actually..." he said, taking another step closer.

I swallowed, looking up at him, the sound of my heart pounding against my chest almost deafening.

He drew so close that our bodies touched. "I think I make you wet."

My breathing came shallow and quick as he brushed my hair over my shoulder. "You think wrong," I lied, turning my attention to my now trembling fingers.

"That so?" He brought his face close to mine, the scruff from his jaw scratching my cheek. Placing his hands against the window, trapping me, waiting until I looked up at him. "You smell good." He inhaled deeply, taking in the scent of the hair at the top of my head, before once more scratching his face against mine, bringing his mouth to my neck. "And you look good. You look different."

"Different than the waitresses who let you fuck them bent over the hood of a car in public?" My brain was telling my mouth to shut up at every word, every *syllable*, but my mouth would not obey.

"Mmm..." He grinned, inhaling at my ear, sending chills down my spine.

I thought he was going to kiss me. Kiss my neck. I didn't even know if I wanted that, or if I wanted him to leave me alone, but when I put my hands against his chest, my effort to push him away was weak at best. As crazy as it sounded, he was right. Having him like this, so close, his breath on me, his scent around me, his big arms caging me in... it made me wet. Even though I knew what he was, what he had done, it made me wet.

But when I felt his tongue on my ear, tracing the contours of it, I jumped to action.

"Stop!"

He traced the outside ridge of my ear and when he reached the lobe, he took it between his teeth and pulled, his bite just hard enough to send an electrical charge straight to my clit. I wasn't the only one affected. I knew it from the steel bar of his cock pressing against my belly.

I made a sound. I wanted to believe it was the sound of my struggle against him, an effort to make him stop, but I wasn't entirely sure if that was the truth. I didn't have to think on it though because he did pull back then, just far enough away that he could look at me, his arms still on either side of me, a cocky grin on his face that said he knew exactly what he was doing to me.

"I think you want me to lick much more than your ear, Mia," he said in that rumbling whisper, staring me down for one more moment before finally releasing me from the cage of his arms and stepping back. "But that'll only happen when I want it, not when you want it," he said, his tone flat as he stepped back and adjusted the crotch of his pants. "And I'm suddenly feeling generous."

The look on his face screamed danger, but all I could do was stand there and wait.

"I'll give you the option of undressing in front of me so I can see that you're not hiding a weapon, or you can turn around, put your hands on the windowsill and spread your legs for me to pat you down. What do you think? Which would you prefer?"

I stared at him, my body doing strange things, the fluttering of my belly, the heat at my core not what I expected to feel. Not what I should feel. I was here against my will, I had to remember that.

His eyes or his hands. I could strip naked for him to ogle me, or I could let him frisk me over my clothes. I figured naked would leave me at my most vulnerable, so, without taking any more time to dwell, I turned, placed my hands on the windowsill and waited.

"I'll be honest," he began, nudging my legs wider. "I wasn't sure which I preferred, but either way, it's a win for me, isn't it?"

"Get it over with, you prick."

"Such foul language from so sweet a young lady," he said, with a tsk. Then he began his search.

If I'd expected a simple pat down, then I was hopelessly

naïve. There was nothing simple about this man, and I should have known he'd make full use of the opportunity. He started with his fingers in my hair, at my scalp, almost massaging as he *checked* me for weapons. What did he expect, a deadly hair clip?

Once he was satisfied, he moved down over my neck and to my shoulders, then down my arms and up along my ribcage before moving all over my back and toward my belly.

I tensed when his hands slid upward, and when he cupped my breasts, I jumped, reaching to stop him.

"Hands on the windowsill, or you get naked. You chose this, Mia. Remember that."

"I'm not hiding anything. You know you're not doing this for that."

"I don't know anything. Now, what's it going to be?" he asked when my hands remained over his.

"Asshole."

He chuckled, but when I pulled my hands away and lay them flat on the windowsill again, he pinched both nipples hard, hard enough for me to cry out and try to pry his hands off again.

"When you talk to me, you will be respectful."

"I wasn't talking *to* you! Get off, you're hurting me!"

But he only twisted harder, seeming satisfied at my whimper.

"When you talk about me, hell, even when you're *thinking* of me, you will be respectful. I don't have a problem punishing you, Mia," he said, still twisting, tears now slipping from the corners of my eyes.

"Please! You're hurting me!"

But he wasn't through yet because he came to stand

against me, his cock pressing against my back, letting me know just how much he was enjoying this. "I should spank you for having spied on me at all, but I've let that go. Don't make me regret my decision to go easy on you."

"Easy?"

"Because I can assure you, I will enjoy punishing you. I'll enjoy seeing you squirm when I turn you over my knee and spank your bare ass."

"Okay, please... just stop." His breath at my ear, the scruff of his jaw at my neck, his body too close, his words... *shit*. I didn't want to think what those words were doing to me. I couldn't think about how wrong my reactions to him were.

"Put your hands back on the windowsill and say you're sorry," he said, easing his hold a little.

I turned my head just enough so I could see him from the corner of my eye.

"Do it, or I'll make good on my promise to punish you. And I mean really punish you."

I hated him, hated how his perfect blue eyes mocked me, but I knew I had no choice. He was in charge here, there was no getting around that, so I turned away from him and set my hands back down on the windowsill before saying the words he wanted to hear.

"I'm sorry you thought I was disrespectful."

He took his right hand off my breast and smacked my ass so hard, my body jerked forward, my pelvic bone colliding against the windowsill.

"Ow! God! I said what you wanted!"

"Not nearly. Try again. Last chance before I bare your ass and make you truly sorry."

"Fine! I'm sorry. I'm sorry I was rude to you!"

He eased his hold on my nipple then and stepped back

just a few inches. "That'll do. You'll find I'm not unreason-able, Mia."

"No, obviously not," I couldn't help saying, squeezing my eyes shut in anticipation of his response. But he simply chuckled and carried on with his search of my body, hands moving over my hips, my buttocks.

He took more time than he needed there before he slid his arms along the outsides of my legs and brought them back up my inner thighs, squatting down as he needed to, and rising again just as he cupped my sex in his right hand.

I don't know why I wasn't prepared for that, why I didn't expect it, but I didn't. So, when it happened, I stood there, my breath caught in my throat, staring straight ahead at the dusty curtains inches from my face.

Julien began to move his fingers then and even through the thick fabric of my jeans, I could feel his touch as if we were flesh to flesh, biting off the sigh that threatened to spill from my lips.

I looked down at his hand, feeling his breath on me again.

"Please stop," I whispered, my plea barely audible.

I looked at him, saw how the blue of his eyes had dark-ened. What caught and held my attention though wasn't how arousal had changed them, rather, it was the look on his face, the fact that he no longer grinned, no longer mocked. When those eyes met mine, the only way I could describe what I felt was that he *saw* me, and, for the briefest of moments, *I* saw *him*.

He dropped his hand and stepped back abruptly.

"Go have your shower. Door stays open."

I looked after him but he didn't look at me then. Instead, he sat back on the bed, his arm splayed over the headboard, and switched on the TV.

It took me a minute, but I walked to the bathroom and did as I was told. I left the door open and climbed into the shower stall and had the hottest shower I could stand, not allowing myself to touch between my legs... even though the urge to do just that was almost unbearable.

9

JULIEN

I flipped through some channels, not paying attention to anything I saw until she was out of the room and the shower went on. Closing my eyes, I sat up and rubbed a hand over the scruff of my jaw.

Why had I told her what I'd told her in the car? I couldn't figure it out. Couldn't figure out why she bugged me. I wasn't used to feeling like this — or feeling anything at all. I was a hit man. An assassin. A killer. As many jobs as came from society's unsavory, there came an equal number from sources thought to be good, law abiding. Law creating. I didn't care who booked my services, as long as they paid. And besides, good or bad, they all died the same. Scared fucking shitless when they figured out what was about to happen to them.

Was it that she was an innocent? Is that what was fucking with me?

No. No one was innocent. It wasn't humanly possible. It would be best for me to remember that the next time I looked into those big green eyes.

I glanced at the bathroom, watching steam pour from

the open doorway, and rose to my feet. "Hope you're not using all the hot water."

The sound of my voice must have startled her because she jerked, the outline of her body visible through the fogged up glass door. I collected her clothes from the bathroom, picking out her panties, and tucking them into my pocket.

"Wrap it up," I called out over my shoulder as I exited the bathroom. I tucked her things into a dresser drawer and set the handcuffs on the nightstand.

The TV was still on and I turned up the volume before returning to the bathroom to open the shower door and switch off the water myself when she hadn't yet done what she was told.

"Hey! I still have shampoo in my hair. And get out!"

I shook the water off my arm and looked her over before holding out a towel and gesturing for her to step out.

She grabbed the towel and covered herself as best she could, trying to shield herself from my view. Her hair hung all the way down her back and looked black now that it was wet. She did this thing with her mouth and I saw the one dimple on her right cheek. I hadn't seen that yet. Mia hadn't smiled once.

Shifting gears, I looked her over. She had a cute little figure, petite for her height but a little too skinny in my opinion. Still, I appreciated the glimpse of her ass before she got the towel around herself. It was the cushiest part of her, more generous than I expected given her slight frame. That was a plus. I turned her, making her walk in front of me, thinking how nicely the little mounds would bounce when I spanked them. And I was sure she'd give me ample opportunity to do just that often — and soon.

"Let go of me." She struggled against me, but I held tight.

"To the bed, come on."

"Why? You said you wouldn't..."

"Relax. I need a shower. I have a feeling you might wander off while I'm in there." I sat her down and pulled both pillows out to rest them against the headboard. "Lie back."

"No."

"Lie. Back."

"At least let me get dressed first."

I smiled as I let my gaze travel over her, taking in toned arms holding that scrap of a towel tight to her chest, her sleek, wet thighs nicely muscled, her feet small, delicate... fragile.

"I prefer you naked. Gives you less incentive to try anything. Now lie back, Mia, arms over your head. I'll even leave the TV on for you."

She looked around the room, then at me, and I knew that *she* knew she was out of options.

"I'll tell you what, do this without a struggle and I'll uncuff you before we go to sleep tonight."

"I promise, I won't..."

"Last chance before I make you."

Although reluctant, she laid back and extended her arms over her head. I slid the cuffs around one of the bars of the headboard and linked her wrists.

"Why aren't we going to the airport yet?" she asked. "I thought you'd want to get me back to Jason fast. You know, collect your money."

I looked at her, her eyes not quite defiant, but clever, trying to read me, to figure me out, looking for weakness. It's what I would do if I were her. She wasn't a coward, even though she was afraid.

I looked away from those eyes and picked up the remote to switch the channel, making a show out of going through all seven of them.

"Only Italian TV," I said, tossing the remote on the foot of the bed. "Be quiet. If you're not, first thing I'll do when I get out here will be to roll you over onto your belly and whip your ass. Got it?"

"I'd scream if you did that. Someone would hear me then."

"Nah," I said, chuckling, pulling my t-shirt over my head, not missing how her eyes raked over my chest, pausing to study each of the tattoos that marked me. "Hotel's pretty empty, and our floor certainly is. Told the front desk clerk you're loud when we fuck."

She had no comeback, and I had to laugh at how red her face turned.

"Behave, Mia."

A shower would be good. A cold one. Stripping off my jeans, I climbed into the stall and switched on the water, which started out hot, but within moments, was lukewarm at best. She'd used up all the hot water. For a moment, I pictured myself punishing her for it, but I had a feeling Mia St. Rose would give me even better reasons to spank that ass. At least in the time I had her before taking her to her brother. She wasn't mine to keep.

Switching off the shower, I climbed out to find there was only one hand towel left. I smiled and walked out into the bedroom.

"What are you doing?" she exclaimed, sitting up higher on the bed, the movement pushing the towel to expose one breast which she tried to cover with her elbow.

She dragged her gaze away, or at least attempted to, but I marched up to her and took hold of one corner of the towel.

"I need to dry off and you've used the one towel, as well as all the hot water. Lift up."

"No, fuck y…" she paused, obviously remembering our earlier conversation. "There was a hand towel. You can use that."

I simply shook my head and yanked on the towel, swiping it out from under her, her body jerking to the side with the swift movement. I looked at her as I wrapped it around my waist, my cock already hardening at the sight of her bound naked on the bed.

She pulled her legs up to cover herself, sitting up higher on the bed, keeping her legs close together so as not to reveal more than she intended.

I stepped closer and gripped my erection. Her eyes followed the movement, widening as they did.

"You make me hard, Mia. Seeing you like this, naked and bound, makes me hard."

She only stared up at me, tightening up even more.

"You said you wouldn't hurt me."

I shook my head. "No, I said I *would* probably hurt you. But I wouldn't rape you. When I want to take you, you'll be spreading your legs wide and begging me to fuck you."

"I won't. You're sick."

"You keep saying that, but I keep remembering who hid and watched me fuck a woman not once, not twice, but three times." I sat on the bed and she scooted away as far as her bonds allowed — which wasn't much. "I recall"—I ran my knuckles over her arm, watching the goose bumps rise along her skin—"your hand disappearing somewhere inside your panties while you watched."

Her breath came faster, the pulse at her neck rapid.

"Just a look, Mia. It's my turn."

She screamed when I yanked on her ankle, tugging her over so that she lay flat on her back. I clamped a hand over her mouth, her eyes growing wider as she stared at me while making little muffled sounds against my hand.

"Be still and be quiet. I just want to have a look, understand?"

She shook her head, struggling, and I pushed on her mouth harder, pressing her head into the pillows, moving my hand up just a little to close her nostrils and block off her oxygen supply altogether. She really panicked then, and I clamped one knee over her thighs, watching her face as she fought, her eyes wild. Somehow, I always remained calm at this moment, just watching my victims.

She wasn't a victim though. I wasn't going to kill her.

"Still and quiet. Understand?"

She nodded violently and I removed my hand. She gasped for breath, trying to pull her legs up. I stood, allowing her to.

"I couldn't breathe," she said, turning her face into her arm.

"I know."

She stopped at that, as if she were surprised. I guess she'd thought it was an accident.

"Now, stretch yourself back out. I want to see you."

Her mind was working, trying to process. I suppose I could have helped her, but I didn't want to. Instead, I waited, patiently watching until she stretched her legs out, laying flat on the bed.

"Good girl."

She was trim, with a small piercing through her belly button. Her nipples hardened beneath my gaze and I could feel her eyes boring into me as I looked her over, pausing at her pussy before continuing down her legs, her thighs, returning my gaze to the dark patch of neatly trimmed hair. I preferred shaved bare. I'd have to remedy that.

"Pull your knees up and spread them, feet flat on the bed."

"Please, Julien."

I looked at her, contempt and confusion at her knowing my name. "Don't say my name."

She nodded, a tear sliding down the side of her face as she pulled her knees up.

I sat down on the bed, taking her left leg wider. She kept her gaze averted. I took in her pretty little pussy, the pink lips that were slightly parted and already glistening.

"I smell you, Mia. I smell your arousal."

She pressed her face into her arm, but not before I saw the tears collected in her eyes. I turned my attention back to her sex, reaching to touch that softest flesh where the curve of her buttock met her inner thigh. She gasped and closed her knees, her gaze snapping back to me.

"You said you'd just look."

"Shh. Open." I waited for her to do as I said, but I kept my fingers on her as I did, sliding them up to the hair, just brushing against the flesh covering her nub, causing her to gasp. "Open your legs."

She did, slowly, and with both hands, I pulled her lips apart, exposing her swollen clit, pink and glistening with moisture.

"You have a pretty pussy," I said, closing her knees and turning her to her side. "Roll over and get up on your knees."

"Why?"

"Because I want to see."

She shook her head.

"You know what I've been thinking about ever since I caught you spying? I've been thinking about what you'd look like on your hands and knees before me, your ass high in the air, just for me."

She whimpered, her scent stronger, her arousal growing. She could deny it all she wanted, but I could smell how turned on she was.

"I want to see that ass of yours spread before me, Mia, see your little asshole, see if it's as pretty as I imagined it."

"Please, don't make me."

"I'm not making you. You want this. You want to show me your ass. You're just as turned on as I am. I can smell it, I can see it. Now, show me. You can bury your face in the mattress if it makes it easier to pretend it's not happening, but you will show me."

With a little more *encouragement* from me, she rolled over, climbing up onto her knees, her face buried in the blankets, her hips lifted high, her ass cheeks spreading to reveal everything to me.

My cock throbbed and I dropped the towel, climbing up between her knees, pushing her legs wider.

She tensed, and I rubbed her back with one hand while gripping my cock with the other.

"Shh. I'm not going to hurt you. I just want to see." I rubbed my length, smearing the pre-cum into my palm and along my shaft, imagining it was her wetness, her cunt hugging my cock. She turned her head and I met her gaze while I slowly rubbed my cock, allowing her to watch, to see.

"You have a pretty cunt, Mia, a pretty asshole, just like I imagined." I rubbed my length a little faster, touching the tip of my cock to one buttock. She didn't startle, instead, she remained still, watching, seeming enthralled.

"I wonder how you taste, how that dripping pussy tastes, that tight little asshole."

Before she could process, I leaned down and slid my tongue over her pussy, the tip of it just finding her clit, causing her to gasp as I circled it, all the while rubbing my cock as I licked the length of her sex.

She shuddered as I tasted that glistening pink all the way up to her asshole, where I circled that tight ring. This time, her moan made me smile and I returned my attention to that swollen nub.

She widened her stance and I closed my mouth around her clit, sucking hard, hearing her breath hitch, her sweet little moans. I straightened, closing one hand over her clit and rubbing hard, feeling like I was about to explode.

Bringing my cock closer to her ass, the tip of it just touching, her breath came fast and hard as she cried out, my cock pulsating in my fist, streams of semen streaking her ass, her back, dripping down over her asshole, her cunt. I pumped the last of my seed onto her, closing my eyes as I shuddered, one hand soaked with her juices, the other with my own, and when I sat back, her eyes met mine for an instant before she turned her face into the mattress, hiding herself from me once more, hiding her tears and her shame from me.

10

MIA

I lay flat on the bed, on my stomach, my wrists still bound over my head. Julien climbed from the bed and switched off the TV. I heard water running and when he returned, he sat back down and cleaned me with a warm washcloth. He didn't speak — neither of us did — and his touch was gentle.

When he was finished, he unlocked my wrists.

"Lift up."

I did and he pulled the blankets out from under me. When our eyes met, I looked at him, trying to understand what had just happened, how I'd come like I had, how I'd been so thoroughly aroused by him, my captor, the man who would deliver me to Jason. The man who would have killed me if it hadn't been for Jason. I wondered about that. It seemed so impossible.

But there were no answers in his eyes, only more questions. The hardness that had been there all along had made space for something else, allowing for an almost imperceptible hint of vulnerability. Perhaps of confusion.

"Lie down, Mia."

I did, and he pulled the blankets over me.

"I'm not going to cuff you, but if you try anything, I will punish you. Understand?"

"Would you have killed me if those men hadn't come into my apartment when they did?" I asked as he stood. "When you figured out I might be worth something?"

He rubbed the palm of his hand over his mouth, watching me. Then he reached to turn off the lamp by my side of the bed, but remained watching me from the dim light of the other lamp.

"I don't know if you want me to answer that."

Lowering my gaze, I shook my head. "No, I guess I don't."

I already knew the answer.

He walked over to the other side of the bed and when he climbed in, I scooted away, gripping my pillow hard.

"Now, that's not very nice after what we just shared," he taunted, an arm wrapping across my belly and pulling me back toward him.

"What are you doing? Let me go."

"I guess I'm a cuddler after all," he said.

"Let me go!"

His grip tightened and he brought his mouth to my ear. "That's no way to act after I licked your pussy and made you come." He squeezed as if to make his point. "Was it like you imagined? Was it as good as when you watched?"

"Fuck you, Julien. I hate you."

"You'll pay for that tomorrow," he said, lying back down but keeping his arm around me. "Get some sleep."

I closed my eyes, crying a little, trying to do it as quietly as I could. If he heard me, he didn't comment. What I'd seen in his eyes after he'd cleaned me had been an unexpected glimpse into a side of him I imagined he didn't show very often. I wondered if he knew I'd seen it actually, that vulnerability. He wasn't a nice man. I didn't fool myself on that account.

He was a hit man. I had to remember that.

I wondered how many women he'd killed, how many men. Would I someday ask? Did I want to know? Of that I wasn't certain.

The room was quiet, and if there were any cars passing, I couldn't hear them. I'd planned to make my move that night, to try to get away from him, but with his arm around me, he'd know. He hadn't nodded off yet; his body was still tense, and his breathing wasn't that of a sleeping man.

I tried to think, to weigh my options. As far as I could see it, I had two: either manage to escape him, or tell him about the million, see if he would help me if I paid him. It would be double what Jason was offering. Would he do it? Would he help me? Well, he was a mercenary. He would help himself and half a million was better than a quarter of a million. On that logic, the answer was yes. I knew Jason would hurt me, there was no doubt of that. He was consumed by hate and vengeance. I needed to do whatever I could to stay out of his grasp.

I didn't fight sleep when I started to drift as Julien relaxed behind me. I closed my eyes and let it come. The clock wasn't on my side of the bed when I woke to a strange sound, my mind still fuzzy from sleep. It took me a minute to figure out where I was in the dark room, but when I felt movement beside me, I remembered. Turning slowly, I watched Julien from the slight light of the moon that slipped through the slit between the curtains. He had tossed the blankets off and was covered in sweat, his lips moving, mumbling words I couldn't make out. He was speaking in a mix of Italian and English, and his brow was furrowed. He tossed, turning in my direction, and when he opened his eyes, I gasped. But he closed them again quickly, still asleep.

I looked around for my clothes, for his clothes, and slowly climbed out of the bed. He didn't notice, still tossing and turning, becoming more agitated by the minute. Part of me wanted to help him, to wake him out of this nightmare, but the logical part of me told me to run. I opened one of the drawers in the dresser, keeping one eye on him as I slid it out as quietly as possible, but it was empty.

"No!"

I jumped, clutching my chest, thinking I'd been caught. But he was still asleep, even as he cried out. Forcing myself to open the second drawer and ignore him, I found it, too, empty.

"Leave him alone!"

This time, there was violence in his words and I froze, unable to turn away from him.

"Charlie! No!"

I watched, hesitating. He kept thrashing about, calling out again, his voice angrier and angrier, and something made me go to him.

"Julien." I whispered.

Mumbling in Italian, he called out that name again. Charlie.

"Julien, wake up. You're having a bad dream." When he wouldn't, I touched my hand as lightly as I could to his arm, but as soon as I did, his eyes flew open, their blue depths bright, wild, shining in the dark of the room. His hand closed around my throat and he leapt from the bed, pushing me into the wall, the force of it knocking the cheap print that hung there to the floor, making the glass crack.

"Wake up! It's me. It's Mia. Wake up, Julien!" My hands

fisted around his forearm but it was impossible to pull him off as he raised me off my feet, cutting off my breath.

"Julien!" I tried one last time, struggling, unable to breathe.

He stilled, finally, staring at me, and I watched in terror as he slowly registered who I was, where we were. He let me down, his eyes still on me while I sucked in air, clutching my throat. He looked so strange. I couldn't read what was in his eyes at all, but he kept them on me, staring at me as if really seeing me for the first time. He touched a hand to my hair, keeping me pinned to the wall all along, my breathing still uneven as my heart pounded.

He didn't say a word, merely watching me as he caressed my hair, his hand heavy as it ran along the side of my head, making me wonder if he wasn't at least partially still asleep.

"Julien?" Fear made a quaking whisper of my voice.

He tilted my face up to his, closing the space between us until our chests touched. Confused emotion flashed in his eyes, and I watched them, watched *him*, but when he pressed his mouth over mine, I made a sound, unsure myself what was happening. My hands went to his chest and pushed, but they made no impact at all, and after a moment, I yielded to him, surrendering, my lips softening, his grip relaxing as he kissed me, my mouth opening to his tongue, my body responding to his touch, his kiss. He moved his hand from my hair to cup one breast, fingernails scratching at my nipple, the sound of my cry swallowed up by his kiss. His cock pressed against my naked belly, the hard length making me want him, and I found myself reaching up to his shoulders, one hand wrapping around the back of his head, pulling him to me.

At that, he turned us, breaking the kiss, leaving me gasping, wanting more. Laying me on the edge of the bed, he pushed my legs up and spread them wide, my knees bending on either side of me. One momentary glance at my pussy was the only instance his eyes left mine and when his thick cock penetrated my too tight passage, I cried out, the pain startling. But he only closed his mouth over mine again, kissing me, eyes open as he fucked me hard, with calculated thrusts that penetrated deep, stretching me to make me take him, my clit rubbing against his belly, the rough hair there, his cock thickening.

My breath hitched and I couldn't kiss him back, but realized he'd stopped kissing me. Our mouths touched, breath mixed, heat and the sound of fucking, of his cock slamming in and out of my wet pussy, the intimacy of a fucking so savage, so ferocious, arousing me to heights I'd never imagined possible, and when he throbbed inside me and pushed my arms over my head, his hands hard around my wrists, I came. I came at the same time as he stilled, his eyes even bluer, if that were possible, as orgasm consumed him and he emptied inside me, sweat dripping on me, mixing with my own when he laid his weight on me, his mouth at my ear, the breathing heavy and hard.

We lay like that for some time, neither of us speaking, until I felt him slide out of me, his cum slippery on my thighs as he stood, looking down at me, his eyes unreadable.

He turned away then, opening one of the dresser drawers and pulling out my clothes. He tossed them onto the bed without looking at me. "Get dressed. We're going." His voice was hoarse and raspy. He gathered his own things and walked toward the bathroom.

"Can I wash?" I asked.

"No."

He closed the bathroom door and I stood there, looking

at the space where he'd just been, watching the closed door, hearing the water run.

I could have run then. I should have. But I didn't.

Instead, I took the sheet off the bed and wiped the residue of his seed off me before gathering up my clothes and putting them on, noticing — but not caring — that my panties were missing. A few minutes later, he emerged from the bathroom fully dressed. He'd run water through his hair and once again he looked like he usually did — hard and unfriendly. When he saw I was dressed, he nodded, then took me by the arm, leading me out the door toward the stairs. We went out the side entrance and straight to the car. I climbed in and fastened my seatbelt. He didn't cuff me this time and we resumed our drive.

It wasn't until the sun rose over the horizon some time later that he finally spoke — though he still refused to look at me.

"Why didn't you run?"

"I... don't know."

Silence again as a deep sienna burnt the sky.

"You didn't use a condom," I said.

His mouth tightened. "I'm clean. I always use condoms. This was the first time I didn't. Are you clean? And protected?"

I paused and he glanced at me with raised eyebrows.

"Yes." I was clean and I wouldn't get pregnant if that was what he was worried about. "Who's Charlie?" I asked, ready for his wrath.

But it didn't come. Instead, he sighed and glanced at me once before returning his attention to the road. "My brother."

Brother?

I couldn't imagine him having a brother, a family.

"He's dead. He hanged himself when he was fifteen."

"Oh, God, Julien." I reached out to touch his arm, but he flinched and I pulled back.

He looked at me then. "I don't need your pity." The way he said it was flat, without spite, devoid of virtually any emotion at all.

"It wasn't pity."

He didn't respond to that, driving in silence.

I wanted to know more. I needed to know more. This man who terrified me was suffering. I didn't know if some sick masochistic side of me wanted to help him or what, but I needed to hear his story, to understand his pain.

"Are you taking me to your childhood home?" I asked, knowing it then, knowing we weren't going to an airport.

He glanced at me as if surprised I knew. He nodded once, his lips tight. I wasn't going to get any more answers now, but what I'd learned was more than I ever imagined I would. This man, this beautiful, deadly man, was three-dimensional, had layers of pain just like the rest of us. But I still had to remember that he was a ruthless killer. I couldn't romanticize him, make him out to be something he wasn't. I had to remember that he wasn't the good guy. He wasn't the hero.

In fact, he was the villain.

But my mind refused to reconcile that last part. He wasn't really that villain, not quite. I knew that somehow. As strange as it sounded, I knew it.

11

JULIEN

I drove on autopilot. What the fuck had happened back in that hotel room? I hadn't dreamt that dream in a long time. Thought it was over, forgotten. But fuck me, it was like I was watching Charlie do it, watching him throw the rope over the beam, watching him slide his neck into the noose he'd made so fucking expertly.

I pressed on the accelerator. Mia glanced my way, but I was beyond caring.

He'd been fifteen when he'd done it. I'd been a year older than him. The foster care system had fucked us, over and over again, but at least they'd kept us together. I'd thought we could survive it because we had each other.

It was when I was told I would be moved, that we wouldn't be together anymore, that he finally did it.

The couple who had taken us in, the last one, had seemed okay at the beginning. Nice. They'd paid special attention to Charlie right from the start. If I hadn't had my head up my own ass, I might have seen when things changed, when the abuse started. He never said a word to me though. He just grew more and more quiet.

I was the one who found him. He'd done it in the closet in the attic. I still wasn't sure for how long he'd been planning it, and some part of me was still angry at him for not having talked to me. For not having told me. But he'd left a note for me in my schoolbag. That was when I knew for sure. The man who'd adopted us had been abusing him for two years. His bitch wife had known about it too, but she'd just looked the other way.

I wiped the back of my hand across my nose and shook my head. I hadn't been able to save Charlie but I had avenged his death. They'd been my first murders, our 'guardians'. They were the reason for the tattoo Mia had asked me about at the restaurant the other day.

Mia.

Fuck.

She sat with her hands in her lap looking out at the road, not talking. I bet she had a thousand and one questions. She baffled me. She could have run. She could have gotten out, but she hadn't.

"What did your stepbrother do to you?"

"What?" Her head snapped around, confusion wrinkling her brow.

"What did he do to you that's got you on the run now? Why did he go to prison, and why is he after you now?"

"His family laundered money for crooks. That's why he went to prison."

"No, his father laundered the money. Jason St. Rose didn't go to prison for that. At least they couldn't find anything linking him. Not yet anyway. All I know is it was your testimony that put him away, but you were a minor at the time and the file is sealed. What did he do to you?"

She looked out the window, shaking her head once, then

turning back to me. "I'm coming into some money which he thinks belongs to him."

Well, this just got more interesting.

"What money?"

She studied me as if weighing her options. "My sister left me a million dollars in her will. I can't claim it until I'm twenty-five and then I have to do so within a month — or I lose it."

"A million dollars?"

"Guilt money."

"But money nonetheless. Tell me about the guilt."

"No."

"What did you do, Mia?"'

"I didn't do anything. In fact, that was the point. It was to buy my silence, my sister's silence. And our obedience. She just felt guilty about it afterwards and didn't spend a fucking penny apparently. And I, obviously, didn't stay silent for long."

"You're angry at her?"

She shrugged a shoulder and looked away. "It doesn't matter. She's dead."

"It does matter."

"You still angry at Charlie?" she asked, surprising me. I wondered if she'd meant to do it, to ask that question to piss me off. But it didn't, somehow.

I wasn't even sure she expected an answer or even wanted one — but she was getting one.

"Yeah, I am in fact."

I exited the highway to begin the ascent to the village where I'd been born. I hadn't been there in a long time and seeing it at the top of the hill, I was glad it was still some distance away. I needed time to manage the shit that was coming up.

I looked at Mia. "I'm angry because if he'd told me what had been going on, I would have helped him. We would have left together. But he didn't. He shut me out and killed himself instead. So, I'm angry for a whole list of reasons."

Tears reddened her eyes as she listened. "I'm sorry."

I guess I expected more, so I just shrugged a shoulder at her response. "Tell me about this million."

"Sounds more appealing than a quarter of a million to hand me over to Jason, doesn't it?"

"It does." I wouldn't kid myself and say it was the only reason I was asking, but I wasn't about to tell her that.

"I can pay you more than Jason will. I'll double it, what he's offering, if you'll help me get the money. I don't care about what you did... what you do. If you hand me back to Jason, I'm dead. If I can get the money, I can disappear. It's what I want. I'll just disappear and it will be like you and I never met, like I never saw you with that woman. The will stipulates that I have to go in person to sign the paperwork in order to claim the money. The attorney who is executing it is my step-father's attorney and it was written in a way that if I don't claim it within a month of my twenty-fifth birthday, it goes to Jason and Allison."

"Who's Allison?"

"Jason's sister. She's okay. I still have contact with her."

I glanced at her. "She's *okay*? How is she *okay*? She stands to gain half a million dollars if you don't show up — or you turn up dead — and you think she's *okay*?"

Mia looked confused, as if she'd not once thought about that possibility. But then she shook her head. "No, Allison's not like that. She's afraid of him too." She paused before adding: "She knows what he's capable of."

"And what is it he's capable of, Mia?" She wanted to tell me. I just needed to help her along. And besides, I did have some idea. It didn't take a genius to figure it out.

"A lot of things."

I nodded. That was fine, I'd wait. "Well, just be smart. Money is a greater motivator than anything else to most people."

"Not everyone's a mercenary."

"Be careful, Mia."

She paused, her eyes on me. "Is that where we're going?" She craned her neck to look up at the hilltop village.

"Yes. It's called Pitigliano."

"It's pretty."

I only nodded. It was pretty.

"So will you help me?"

"I'm still considering. Do you have some proof of the million?"

She shook her head, exhaling loudly. "Yes. Or I did. It's back at the hotel in my suitcase."

"Well, isn't that convenient."

"Look, all you have to do is take me to get the money. If I'm lying, which I'm not, you can turn me in to Jason then and collect your quarter of a million. But if you're patient, that quarter gets doubled. You can't tell me you don't want that. I mean, it's kind of obvious, right?"

I chuckled, taking the last curve. "Yeah, but it means I have to put up with your smart mouth."

"Screw you."

"See what I mean?" I drove into the village. It had been years since I'd been here. I hadn't even called my grandmother to tell her I was coming. Not that I owed her a call. I paid her well to keep the house up. Hell, I'd barely talked to her at all in the last five years.

My grandmother had had my mom young, and out of wedlock — which was not done here. She'd gotten married some years later, but that hadn't worked out for her either and she'd been on her own ever since. If she hadn't been a drunk, what happened to Charlie wouldn't have happened. She'd have become our guardian. Everything would have been different if she'd wanted us. If she'd been able to take care of us. But she hadn't, and that was that.

The past was dead, as was my brother.

I parked the car as close as I could to the house, but we'd have to walk a little ways. I turned to Mia, watching her watching me.

"All right, so the math is obvious. I keep you alive, get you to where you need to be by your birthday, and I get half a million. Where is it you need to be, anyway?"

"Philadelphia."

"Okay. How long is it to your birthday exactly?"

"Two weeks from now." She rolled her eyes as she said it, but I could tell she was nervous.

"I have one condition."

"What condition?"

"I make all the calls. You do as you're told in all things, and that's it."

"What kind of *calls*?"

That made me grin. "Any kind." I knew what she was talking about, just as surely as I knew her confusion about what she wanted, about how she reacted to me. "Are you prepared to accept that?"

She studied me for a moment, and I watched her choosing her words, trying to find a way to ask what she wanted to ask, but without seeming to care. She *did* care though. The bright red of her face told me that.

"Do you mean... I..." She glanced away, then looked at me once more. "What happened at the hotel..."

This was too good. "*Any* kind."

"You can't..."

"Did you come when I licked your cunt, Mia?"

Her mouth fell open, her eyes going wide, her face flaming red.

"Did you come when I fucked you this morning? Because I think you did."

"I... You can't—"

"Did you come?" I asked, trying to keep her off balance. People liked to hide from the truth when the truth didn't serve them. I'd be damned if I was going to let her do that.

"I... that doesn't mean—"

"Did you come? Yes or no? It's a simple question, requiring a simple answer."

"You're a fucking prick."

"That's twice now that you've been disrespectful. Since I've been counting, that is. We'll address that in a minute. For now, answer my question."

"Fine. Yes." She looked out her window, and bit her lip to keep her mouth shut. It made me smile, her defiance. She wanted this, but wanted to be made to give it.

Screw that. She'd face who she really was.

"I won't take anything you don't give me — but I can guarantee you'll be giving it. Do you agree to my condition?"

"I don't have a choice."

"Sure you do. Your stepbrother is your other choice."

"Like I said, no choice."

"I could really use a cup of coffee." I raised my eyebrows, waiting on her to say it.

"Fine. Yes. I agree."

Smiling, I opened the car door. "Welcome to Pitigliano, Mia."

12

MIA

*J*ulien took my hand as we walked through the village. He didn't hold it as if it were a form of affection. He did it to keep me with him without it looking obvious. Not that it mattered. It was still early in the morning, not quite ten o'clock, and there were only a few people on the streets.

I was so taken with the ancient village that I tripped more than once on our way up the uneven street. Julien caught me each time, although he did mumble something about watching where I was going.

The few people we passed looked at us and I smiled at them. I was more interested in how they reacted to Julien, than to me. He kept his gaze straight ahead, the tension rolling off his body. When we got to a café, the mouthwatering smell of freshly baking bread made my stomach growl but Julien seemed unaffected by it. He took a deep breath and walked inside, his hand growing clammy around mine.

"Grandmother," he said to the woman behind the bar

who stood with her back to us, her hand on the counter, a cigarette smoking between her fingers .

The woman turned from the TV she was watching to face us. At first, she looked shocked to see him, but then a smile crept along her face and she came around the counter, cigarette in hand, talking loudly as she wrapped her arms around Julien in a familiar hug. He didn't let go of my hand and he didn't hug her back. Either the woman didn't notice, or didn't care. She spoke in rapid Italian, extravagant hand gestures accompanying her speech, pausing now and then, hugging him a second time before finally quieting and step-ping back, looking at me with a smile on her face. She said something to me in Italian, but Julien replied before I could tell her I didn't understand what she'd said. What he said, however, wiped that smile right off the older woman's face.

"Mia, this is my grandmother, Gianna."

"Nice to meet you," I said, holding out a hand.

Gianna turned to put her cigarette out in an ashtray on the bar and reached her hand out to take mine. But a moment later, she gave Julien a look and pulled me into a hug, speaking fast in Italian. She then stepped back and looked me over. "Mia. Nice to meet you." Her English was heavily accented, but it was better than my Italian and I found I liked this woman. She wasn't afraid of Julien.

I smiled and she went behind the counter to make coffee.

"Sit," Julien said in his usual charming manner. He pointed at a barstool.

Gianna pushed an espresso toward me.

"Your grandmother seems very warm." My comment was directed at Julien even though I looked at and thanked Gianna. "Not what I'd expect, considering," I mumbled as I sipped my drink.

Julien leaned in close. "That's three," he whispered into my ear. He gave me a smirk and picked up his coffee.

I watched as Gianna talked with Julien who listened to the woman in silence. He was tense, I could tell, but I wasn't sure if his grandmother picked up on it at all. Gianna opened the cash register, took out a key and set it on the counter. She slid it over to Julien.

"I will send clean sheets this afternoon," she said, smiling at me sweetly.

Two older gentlemen walked into the café then and she smiled at them. Julien too turned and I watched as one of the men paused, then strode over to him with a wide, warm smile, greeting him with a pat on the back and some murmured words in Italian. Julien shook his hand, but he barely managed a smile. All I caught in the exchange was one word: Charlie. I watched Julien when the man said it. The man's tone became somber at the mention of Charlie, but Julien's face went rigid.

"Are you finished?" Julien asked me.

I drank the last sip of my coffee and nodded. He said goodbye to his grandmother and the old men and I stumbled through my farewells in rudimentary Italian.

"The house is a little farther up the hill." His tone was completely different from the one I'd come to know thus far. The hardness was gone, replaced by something else, something old and weary — and perhaps hurt. When he slowed and glanced to his right, I followed his gaze. It was a cemetery. Something in the moment made me squeeze my hand around his, and when I did, he turned to me, his eyes questioning, a vulnerability in them I hadn't seen before. I didn't ask, but I had a feeling his family was buried there.

Without speaking, he led the way down a few more streets and up the stairs to a pretty, ancient-looking wooden door. Unlocking it, he switched on the light. Even though it was daytime, the house was dark and musty, as if it had been closed up for a long time. I stood in the entrance while he moved to the next room and opened a window before pushing the wooden shutters open. I followed him, smiling as sunshine filled the small rooms. He pulled the dusty, yellowed covers off the furniture to reveal very old furniture, the seats of which were worn, the floral pattern fading in places. Rings marked the wood of the coffee table and a stack of saucers sat on a crocheted doily on one corner. There wasn't anything extravagant or modern here.

"Wow, this is amazing," I said when I went to one of the windows. The house was situated along one of the cliffs, and the view across the valley below was vast and incredible.

He walked into the small kitchen and returned holding a cigarette and a lighter. He met me at the window and put the cigarette to his mouth, flicking the lighter twice before igniting a flame. I watched as he lit the cigarette, listening to the sound of it burn as he inhaled. Leaning out the window, he exhaled, physically relaxing as he did. I realized he'd done it in the restaurant parking lot too. It seemed strange that he smoked, a man who was physically quite healthy, totally in control of everything. It was almost a weakness.

"Why do you smoke?"

After another long drag, he took the cigarette from his mouth and looked at it, holding that breath. He then stubbed it out on the outside wall, tossing the butt away before turning to me. "Trying to quit." He went toward the living room.

"So, this is where you were born?"

He grunted his answer with a short nod. This was hard for him, I could hear and see it.

"Your grandmother seems happy to see you."

He just raised his eyebrows and gave me a strange non-smile before moving to the stairs. "Guilt," he said, stopping on the first step and watching me as he said it. "Come upstairs."

Guilt.

I guessed we had more in common than either of us had originally thought.

I followed him up the stairs, my heart beginning to beat a little faster at what was to come, my belly suddenly filled with butterflies. The worst part though was that I didn't know what I wanted. I should have wanted him to leave me alone. I should have wanted to get away, even if Julien claimed he would help me.

But all I wanted was to follow him up those stairs.

The floors throughout the house were tiled, though worn carpet could be seen here and there. The stairs were uneven, the second story consisting of one bedroom and a small bathroom.

"Can I?" I asked, pointing to that little room.

He gestured for me to go ahead and went into the bedroom to wait. I closed the door and, after opening the tiny window in the bathroom, looked at my reflection in the mirror.

I wore no makeup and a handful of freckles dotted my nose from being out in the sun a few days ago without sunscreen. It was early spring and although it wasn't really warm yet, I had managed to get a little sun. That was days ago though — before I'd ever thought I'd actually meet the man whom I'd watched from my hotel window.

Turning the tap, I splashed cold water onto my face and rinsed my mouth. I combed my fingers through the tangles of my hair, needing a brush to get the knots out, but, settling on a long braid for now, I headed back to meet Julien.

He'd opened the window and was sitting on the one armchair in the room, waiting for me. The look on his face set the hair on the back of my neck standing on end, and I tried to remind myself who this man was, *what* he was. But it was as though my mind was shutting that out.

"Undress, Mia."

My clit was the first thing to react to his words, but my brain thankfully took over.

"Why?"

"Because I want you naked. Undress."

I shook my head, a small, uncertain movement.

He grinned, and shifted so that he uncrossed his legs and leaned forward, resting his elbows on his knees and steepling his fingers.

"Mia."

I stood listening, holding my hands behind my back to hide how they shook.

"Do you remember our conversation in the car not an hour ago?"

I nodded, sweat beginning to form under my arms, across my forehead.

"This is one of the calls I get to make to which you agreed. Do you need me to make you strip? You have a punishment coming already so I'll just add on to it if I have to strip you myself. But you'll be naked, one way or the other."

"Punishment?" We hadn't discussed that.

He smiled, nodding while raising his eyebrows.

"Why?"

He shrugged a shoulder. "Doesn't need to be a reason other than it will please me to spank that ass of yours. But in this case, it's your disrespectful attitude."

"Spank?"

"Strip."

"Julien—"

"Mia."

I watched his face, his eyes, wondering if he was joking — but he wasn't. He leaned back, crossing his right leg over his left, as if preparing to watch a show. A striptease.

"I'll ask once more, and if you still refuse, then I'll assume you want me to help you. Undress."

"I…"

He was up on his feet in a flash of movement, and before I could get a scream out, he had his hand over my mouth and pushed me against the wall. With his other hand, he tore my blouse down the middle, swatting my flailing arms away like they were nothing before he turned me to face the wall, pressing me into it with one hand between my shoulder blades. I heard a *woosh* and knew he'd pulled his belt through the loops. For a moment, I thought he'd whip me with it and I screamed, but then he gathered my arms behind me and wrapped the thick leather around my wrists, winding it tight and buckling it before turning me to face him again.

I stared wide-eyed, the look on his face fierce, the pupils of his eyes dilated.

"Shh," he said, his hand at my throat. "No one will come to help you if you scream. You'll just irritate me."

I screamed anyway when I noticed the switchblade he'd pulled out of its case on his jeans, and when I did, he clamped his hand back over my mouth and cut away my bra first between my breasts, then at the straps over my shoulders, the ruined lace falling open, exposing me.

"Shut up. I mean it," he said, taking his hand away but using my own bra as a gag when I opened my mouth. "Better." He stepped back to have a look at me before putting his knife away and reaching for the buttons of my jeans.

I began to mumble behind the gag, tears filling my eyes, suddenly incredibly frightened of this man who I'd been stupid enough to let down my guard with. He was a *killer*. He was a murderer, an assassin. I was so out of my league, I had no idea what I was doing.

He ignored me though, easily keeping me pinned to the wall as he pushed my jeans down to my knees.

"Step out of them," he demanded.

My plea was muffled by my bra, and this time, instead of asking me again, he turned me to face the wall once more and smacked my ass three times. It hurt. He struck hard and when he turned me again and repeated his command, I did as he said, working my legs to pull the jeans off without the use of my hands, and stepping out of them while he held me upright.

I wasn't wearing panties because I hadn't found them earlier, so I now stood before him naked and bound, my bra shoved into my mouth, waiting for his next command.

His eyes raked my body and his breath was hot on my face when he pressed himself to me, his cock a steel rod against my stomach. He kissed my temple and pushed the hair from my face.

"I think you're getting comfortable, Mia. Maybe thinking you know me? That perhaps we have something we've... connected on?"

I shook my head, but he was right — I had thought something.

"I think it's important you know your place, that we set boundaries here and now."

He kissed my face again, this time while pulling his t-shirt over his head with one hand, leaving him naked from the waist up, the ink on his chest and arms the only barrier between us. I couldn't help looking at him, wanting to take in all those markings, wanting to know what each one meant, but when he leaned in close and pulled the makeshift gag from my mouth, I didn't scream. Instead, I took his kiss, wanting him, desiring him even.

This was wrong, this was so very wrong.

"You need to know, Mia," he said, replacing the gag and bringing his face down to my breast, licking it while I watched before taking the nipple between his teeth, biting just hard enough for me to squeeze my eyes shut and groan against the pain. "That I'll take what I want when I want it." He kicked my legs apart, and slid a hand down over my slit, gripping my mound hard. "You see, I know you want it too. Your pussy's wet for me, isn't it?" His fingers slipped through the drenched folds of my pussy.

I closed my eyes when he beamed his victorious grin. But Julien wasn't done yet.

He leaned in, whispering in my ear but never stopping the play of his fingers, his thumb now moving over my clit.

"You want me to take it, don't you? You like it rough, Mia?"

I shook my head, but I wasn't sure it wasn't a lie.

"Your pussy says something else."

He pushed the gag from my mouth again to kiss me, and this time, he didn't replace it. Instead, he walked me over to the bed and sat me down on it, one hand remaining curled in my hair. He looked at me for a while, his hand almost caressing my scalp. Then he pushed me backward so I lay flat on my back, and he knelt between my legs on the floor, his hands on my belly, my breasts.

"I like the taste of your pussy," he said, his eyes locked on mine while he licked it. "I like sucking on this hard little clit," he continued, doing just that, making me gasp, making me lift my hips into his face. One finger slid into my cunt as he licked and sucked and I was ready to explode when he stopped, licking just to the side of my clit, looking at me.

"You want me to make you come?"

I couldn't answer.

"You don't want to want it, I get that. But you do, don't you? I won't judge you, Mia." He slid his finger out of my pussy, tracing it back to the other hole. I pushed away from him when I felt it touch that tight ring of muscle, but he only had to pinch my nipple to make me stop. "You belong to me now, Mia. Every part of you belongs to me until I let you go. It'll be easier for you if you can accept that."

With that, he pushed his finger into my asshole, watching me as I flinched at the intrusion. It hurt at first, but then, he began to rub, to pull his finger in and out while licking my pussy again, his eyes on me, and when he wrapped his lips around my clit and worked a second finger into my ass, I came. I fucking gushed all over his face, his mouth, his tongue, his fingers pumping slowly in and out of my ass, my muscles clamping around them, coming like I'd never come before.

Once the spasms had passed, I opened my eyes to meet his. He wasn't laughing, he wasn't gloating. He simply knelt there, watching me. He slid his fingers out of my bottom then, and turned me over onto my belly. Standing, he undid the belt that bound my wrists.

"Let's take care of that punishment before we continue," he whispered. "Grip the rails of the headboard and don't move your hands."

I watched him double up the belt, and, even knowing what was coming, I did as he said, unable to disobey.

"Now, that's a good girl."

He placed his knee at my back then, pinning me down so that my legs hung off the foot of the bed and my butt was raised slightly.

"You'll feel this even more now that you're ultra sensitive," he said, and as I processed his words, his meaning, he began to whip me, lashing my ass with his belt.

I'd never been spanked before, not by hand or anything else, and the leather of the belt bit into me like fire with each stroke. I struggled, trying to get away. I screamed. I wondered if the entire village could hear my screams, but it didn't matter. I didn't care. It hurt, it fucking *hurt* like hell, but he only continued laying on stroke after stroke until I was spent and weeping, no longer fighting. As soon as I stopped, he did too. I heard the belt drop to the floor and felt when he sat down on the bed, pulling me onto his lap, belly down, rubbing circles over my punished bottom while I wept.

"Why did you do that?" I asked through tears when he lifted me up to cradle me in his arms. Even as I asked, I found myself tucking my arms into myself, into him, almost taking shelter in his embrace.

"Shh," he coaxed. "It's over now, but you needed to know how you'd be punished."

"Why?"

He held me close, one hand caressing my hair. I looked up at him to find him watching me.

"Why?" he asked.

I nodded.

"Because I like it."

With that, he brought his mouth to mine and kissed me

once before sliding me off his lap and setting me on the edge of the bed, my bottom hurting when it made contact with the sheets.

He stood between my legs then and unbuttoned his jeans, pushing the denim and his underwear down, bringing his thick, hard cock inches from my face.

"It's important that you remember, Mia, that although you may think you know me, may think you know my pain, my suffering, you don't. You need to remember that I am a mercenary, like you said." His fingers curled in my hair as he pushed me to my knees. "All you need to know is that I will hold up my end of the bargain, and you had better make sure to hold up yours. You'll do as I say, or you'll be punished every time. Understand?"

I nodded, my eyes moving to his cock, my sex stirring at the sight of it, the scent, the closeness, even given what he'd just done to me. That was the craziest realization of all.

I was turned on, completely aroused.

"Suck my cock, Mia. I want to come down your throat."

I opened my mouth, my eyes on his as he guided himself between my lips, one hand keeping a grip on my hair as he closed his eyes. I sucked, watching him as I did, watching his face, the pleasure there. And when he pushed deeper, I took him as far as I could, sucking harder, still watching him. When he opened his eyes to look at mine, the blue was brighter, shinier. He kept his eyes on mine then until he came, until his cock thickened inside my mouth, throbbing, releasing down my throat, his taste salty, clean, leaving me wanting.

Wanting.

It was so strange that I should want him, but when he slid out of my mouth, pulling me to stand, bringing his lips to mine, that was the only word to describe what I felt.

I wanted him.

He was wrong about one thing though. I did know him. I knew pain. I knew suffering.

And *he* suffered. No matter how hard he tried to make himself appear, I knew he suffered.

13

JULIEN

I watched Mia sleeping. I wasn't getting any myself tonight, so I watched her instead. She lay on her side in the bed and I sat on the armchair there, keeping vigil like some creep. Her mouth was slightly open, and I could hear her soft inhalations of breath. She slept peacefully, not even uttering one word, barely turning over. I'd been sitting here like that for almost an hour and she'd not moved except to curl her little hand over the blanket and tug it closer to her neck.

In a way, I was envious of her restful sleep, but sleep made you vulnerable. It put you on your back.

I stood and went to her, pushing the hair off her forehead before sliding the blanket to her waist. She tucked her arms into her chest, but apart from that, there was no other movement. She was naked but for the comforter that covered her and I looked at her small breasts, perky and round, just a handful. Perfect. Her pretty little nipples hardened now in the cool air. I'd left the window open even though it got cold up here at night. I liked listening to the insects, the birds in the still dark hours of the morning.

She was so freaking vulnerable right now. I could do anything to her, and yet, she slept. Like a fucking baby. Hell, I could smother her in her sleep and she'd be gone. A life over in an instant. A life taken. It was what I did, after all.

Without covering her, I turned and walked out of the bedroom. It was good to remember who I was. And her innocence was so opposite that. Whipping her earlier had felt good, but having her in my arms afterwards, having her cradled so that she lay her head on my chest, almost crawling into me? That was something else. I guess I'd expected her to hate me after the whipping — but her reaction hadn't been that at all.

Why I even gave a shit I didn't know — but I did.

Was I looking for redemption? Did I somehow think saving one life would make up for all the ones I'd taken? They had all deserved to die; I'd never felt remorse over any of the things I'd done. So what the fuck was happening to me now?

I went into the kitchen and switched on the light, opening the drawer where the cigarettes were. I looked at them, but just pushed it closed again. I didn't want a cigarette. I wanted my mind clear of these thoughts, and sitting there idle wasn't helping. *She* wasn't helping.

Hell, she had me fucking scared to sleep. I didn't want that nightmare again, didn't want to see Charlie like that again. Ever.

Fuck.

Her purse sat on the kitchen table and I dumped the contents out. It was all the usual crap: wallet, lipstick, tissues, gum — nothing interesting. Nothing apart from her phone. I picked it up and found two contacts — one for 'Allison,' and another for 'J. Thompson.' Taking out my own phone, I copied both over, then dialed Ryan.

"Julien. What's up?"

"I need you to look up some info on Allison St. Rose for me. She's Jason's kid sister."

"All right, I can do that. She was hardly mentioned in the earlier reports though."

"Well, look again. I want to know how much contact she has with her brother now. And I want to know more about Mia's sister. Tanya? Died in a car crash?"

I could hear Ryan clicking away on his keyboard while I asked. "Yep. Car went over a bridge in New Jersey. Body was never found, but she was declared dead."

"Nothing says suspicious like a missing body."

"Well," Ryan began, still typing fast. "Police report ruled it an accident. Samuel said she'd had some drinks and they'd had a fight. Always interesting."

"That is interesting. How old was she?"

"Not quite twenty-six. Shame too. She was a looker."

"How did she meet Samuel St. Rose anyway?"

It was quiet while he worked. "Typical. She was a prostitute. High end, but still. Probably met him escorting."

"Then he marries her?"

"I'll send over a photo," Ryan said, chuckling.

"What about money? Did she have any?"

"A million was transferred to a fund in her name back when she was eighteen. Doesn't look like she touched it though and"—more typing—"looks like that goes to your girl, unless of course, she doesn't pick it up. Then it reverts to the St. Rose kids, to Jason and Allison. Split right down the middle."

"So, we're talking five hundred grand each on top of the millions they already have? That's why he's got a hit on her?"

That didn't make sense. That much money wouldn't matter to them.

"Hold on, there's more."

Ryan typed while I listened, tapping my foot, impatient. "What more?"

"Give me a minute, man. Okay, the dad owned a dry cleaning business. Several, in fact. He was being investigated for laundering money for some pretty bad people, which we knew about. Ah! Holy hell."

"Go on."

"One of the ledgers went missing a week before Tanya St. Rose's death. I'm guessing it's the real one and I'm guessing the St. Roses want it back bad."

"That so?"

This was getting more interesting by the minute.

"Yep."

"Find me what you can about Allison, Ryan."

"Will do. When are you delivering Mia?"

I looked out the window, up at the stairs. I wasn't going to tell Ryan my plans. Not yet. He'd get his cut, but he didn't need to know about the change in numbers. "Soon."

There was a pause on the other end of the phone, and for the first time in the years I'd known Ryan, that pause made me think.

"I'll be in touch soon," Ryan said finally.

"Thanks."

Ryan was smart, and he thought like a criminal. I'd have to remember the warning I'd given Mia just yesterday. Money was the biggest motivator for most people. That was all there was to it.

I checked the time. It was almost five in the morning. Now was as good a time as any. Grabbing my jacket, I headed out the front door. Town was quiet, as expected. A partial moon lit the way to the cemetery, but I could have made the walk in the pitch dark. Charlie and I would play there when we were kids. I just never expected him to be a permanent resident of the place, not before me at least. He was my kid brother.

My grandmother had gotten her shit together after he died. Too little, too late, but at least she flew his body back to be buried in Italian soil with his parents. She was a tough old lady, my grandmother. And smart. She'd liked Mia, said something about her making an honest man out of me. But I shook my head at that. Mia wasn't my girlfriend. She needed me, and I never turned down the kind of money she was worth. That was all.

A business arrangement. With benefits.

The gate creaked as I pushed it open. There were too many old people in Pitigliano. Not enough work to keep the younger ones here aside from tourism, and Pitigliano wasn't exactly on the beaten path. Which was a good thing as far as I was concerned — but the village would someday die. It wouldn't happen in my lifetime, but it would happen.

Walking along the path, I made my way toward the far corner where my family was buried. I hadn't been here at all since Charlie had been buried. I'd been too pissed off to be anywhere. I'd gotten into drugs and lived on the streets for the first three years. But then I'd gotten smart. I'd started to do what I did so well. I became an assassin.

The three headstones stood lined up in a row, my mom in the middle, my dad on one side of her and Charlie on the other. I paused and took a deep breath before taking the final steps, pulling out some weeds along my father's head-stone before sitting down against the fence. I just sat there looking at them, not sure I wanted to figure out what I was feeling, picking at the grass instead, just looking at the headstones, reading their names. My parents had been happy. They'd been crazy in love, from what I remembered. We'd been a happy family. If we'd stayed in Italy, none of what happened would have happened. But times were hard, and you needed money to live.

I looked up at the sky, pushing down the weight that built in my chest. I stayed a while until dawn began to lighten the sky, waking the first of the birds. I may have dozed off, but it didn't matter. I got up and pulled up three poppies, setting them on each of the headstones.

I didn't look back when I walked out of the cemetery. I went to the house and took some money out of my wallet, leaving a note for Mia to go into town and buy what she needed for clothes since I'd destroyed hers.

Then I lay down on the sofa and closed my eyes.

14

MIA

It was a little past ten in the morning when I woke up. I stretched my arms and opened my eyes. It took me a minute before I remembered where I was. And with whom. But a look around the room told me I was alone.

I'd slept through the night somehow. That hadn't happened in... well, since I'd been on the run. Last night was the first in a long time. Which was strange considering my housemate was a hit man whose original intent had been to kill me. But he wasn't going to kill me now. He was going to keep me alive, in fact. The cost would be half of my inheritance — but that piece would be easier to give up than the other — the part that made me question who I was. Why I was reacting the way I was to him.

What had happened yesterday, what he'd done to me... he'd made me come. He'd whipped me, and he'd made me want him. I'd taken shelter in his arms after he'd punished me. I still felt the residual pain of the whipping when I sat up, a reminder for the next few days, I imagined. What had he said when I had asked him why? He'd wanted to do it? No, he *liked* doing it. I didn't understand that.

I climbed out of bed and picked up my blouse, which was torn. At least he hadn't ripped apart my jeans. I didn't have any other clothes with me. I'd have to keep my raincoat on and just buy something new. Walking quietly to the bathroom, I tried to remember how much cash I had left. Problem was, some of it was in my suitcase — which was at the hotel in Cosenza.

Crap.

I opened the door to the tiny shower, switching on the water, finding a half bottle of shampoo and conditioner in there. The water spurted at first — the shower probably hadn't been used in a while — but after a moment, I had hot water. After locating one of the towels Gianna had sent up to us, I climbed into the stall and closed my eyes, enjoying the warm spray.

Julien had agreed to help me get the money. On the one hand, that was a huge relief. But on the other, it was scary as hell. What would he demand of me in the meantime? What had I agreed to?

I couldn't think about that now though. I needed to call Allison to let her know that I was all right, in case she had heard about the men Jason had sent. She would be worried by now. I thought about what Julien had said about her. He didn't trust her intentions, but that was because of who he was. I had to remember that. He didn't really know Allison.

I wish I knew how Jason had found me. I'd thought I was being so careful, but I was naïve. Julien was right, he was better at this than I was. But I wasn't a criminal like him. Like Jason. I would learn, though, over the next two weeks. I'd learn, and once I got the money, I'd disappear.

But first, I had to survive the next two weeks.

The water cooled a little and I switched it off, feeling better after shampooing my hair. I wrapped the towel around myself and stepped into the hallway, peering down the stairs into the living room. I saw Julien lying on the couch, asleep. I watched him for a minute, so curious about him, but when he moved a little, I quickly went into the bedroom and closed the door. Pulling on my jeans, I picked up my ruined bra and tossed it into the trashcan. I then slipped on my blouse and tied a knot to hold it together at my belly. It would be a cute way to wear it — if I were twelve. Shaking my head, I picked up my shoes and carried them down the stairs, not wanting to wake Julien.

In the kitchen, I found my purse along with a note and some money.

Go into the village and buy some clothes.

J.

I supposed this was the closest to an apology I would get from him.

Slipping my shoes on, I shoved the money into my purse and left the house. The village was small enough that I found my way easily, coming to Gianna's café first. I checked that I was appropriately buttoned up and walked inside to find Julien's grandmother talking to one of the men whom I'd met yesterday, but when she saw me, she threw her hands up, beaming at me, chattering loudly in Italian. I couldn't help but smile back.

Without asking, she made me a cappuccino and set it in front of me, along with a croissant.

"Thank you," I said, picking up the coffee.

"Where is my grandson?" she asked, making a show of looking around me.

"Sleeping on the couch."

She studied me and I realized I'd perhaps given away too

much. I thought back to yesterday, remembering how I'd screamed, embarrassed at the idea she may have heard, that she might know what he'd done to me. But if she did, she didn't let on. Her clever eyes simply regarded me for a moment.

"He went to see his family yesterday," she said, nodding. "About time he is back. He needs to make peace with what happened."

"What do you mean he went to see them?"

"The cemetery. I stop there every morning to speak with them, tell them what's happening in village." She waved her hand in the air to dismiss what she was saying. "Old Italian women are strange, Mia. Pay no mind. Tell me how he is, truly," she asked, with a quick, earnest nod of her head, wanting to draw out any information I could give her.

"I don't know. I'm sorry, we haven't known each other long." I felt my face flush as I said it, thinking about the circumstances that had brought us together.

Her dark eyes studied me, waiting.

"He is angry. I know that much," I said.

She nodded, her face growing sadder, her gaze sliding away. "How long will you stay?"

"A couple of weeks, I think. I'm not sure, really." I finished the pastry and sipped the last of my coffee. Three customers walked in then and Gianna turned her attention to them.

"Mia, stay. Help me later?" Gianna asked as she moved back behind the bar. The woman's eyes seemed to beg me to say yes. "It will be very busy today."

"I can help. First, I need to buy some clothes. My suit-case was... lost."

Her expression told me she didn't buy it, but she pointed

out the door and to the right. "Go to Myra. She is in main square. Tell her Gianna sent you."

"Myra?"

She nodded.

"Okay, I'll be back as soon as I can to help."

I reached into my purse to take out my wallet, but she put her hand on mine to stop me. "It is okay, Mia. You are with Julien. You are family."

I hesitated, but then thanked her and put my wallet away. She was lonely and I could see she was hurting more than she let on. I imagined it had to do with Julien. I would be back to keep her company, at least. I had nothing else to do anyway.

Walking out the door, I headed down in the direction of the square which we'd passed on the way into town the day we arrived. While I did, I picked up my phone and, although I knew it would be late, I dialed Allison. I could at least leave her a voice mail.

But when she picked up after the first ring, I stopped short.

"Mia?" She sounded frantic.

"Allison, what is it?" I asked, suddenly panicked.

"Mia, I heard about the men Jason sent. How did you... are you okay? Where are you?"

"You heard? How?"

There was a pause. "Jason came by again. He was pissed, said you killed two of his men."

"No, it wasn't me. It was—"

You can't tell her.

Why was Jason involving her at all in this? He'd accused her at first of taking my side, calling her a traitor to her own blood. But now, he was telling her he'd sent men after me?

"Mia?"

"I'm here. I'm sorry. It's okay, Allison. I'm fine, and I have someone who's going to help me get the money and disappear where I won't have to ever worry about Jason again."

"Who's helping you?"

"It's a long story."

"Can you trust him?"

"I don't have a choice, Allison."

"I'm worried about you."

"Don't be, it will be fine."

"Where are you?"

I paused, looking up at the wide blue sky. "I can't tell you, but I'm safe. For now."

She sighed deeply. "I won't tell him. I just want to help."

"I know, Allison. I just... it's safer for you if you don't know."

"Tell me who you're there with, in case anything happens to you."

"Nothing's going to happen to me. He'll keep me safe, at least until he gets paid — and he can't do that until I get the inheritance."

"So, you're paying someone?"

"Listen, I have to go." I had to get off before I told her more than I already had. If Jason was now visiting his sister with details of the kidnap plan gone wrong, I couldn't take a chance on her knowing anything — and I'd already said too much.

"Stay safe, Mia."

"You too, Allison."

I hung up the phone and dropped it back into my bag, locating Myra's shop and heading toward it. There were more tourists in the village today, probably because it was the weekend. When I went into the shop, a pretty, young girl looked up from the counter, her eyes moving over me from head to toe before greeting me.

"*Ciao.*"

"*Ciao.* Gianna sent me to see... Myra?" I didn't guess this was a Myra. She definitely didn't look like I imagined a Myra might look.

"Myra is my grandmother. I am Angela. She is not here today, but I can help you. Are you the American here with Julien?"

Although I wasn't surprised that news spread fast in the tiny village, the way she said what she said grated on me. It wasn't meant to sound friendly.

"I am. I'd like a blouse, please." I looked around the shop, quickly picking out two blouses as well as a pretty white linen dress.

Angela led me toward a tiny fitting room with hardly a smile on her face.

"Do you know Julien?" I asked, not sure why I was getting the look of a jealous lover. I certainly wasn't his lover, not by choice anyway. That was true, right?

And besides, how would she know him? He'd not been back in years from what I had gathered.

"Everyone knows of Julien, the prodigal grandson," Angela said when I came out of the fitting room in the dress. "I saw him last night. Looks nice."

I wasn't sure if she was talking about the dress or Julien.

She'd seen him last night? He'd gone out for a drink — he'd told me he would. And certainly, he had no obligation to me, but had he...?

"The dress, or Julien?" I asked without thinking.

Angela grinned, challenge clear in her eyes. "Both."

"I'll take the dress and the blouses. And some of these." I picked up several pair of panties along with two bras in my size, and handed them all over to her. "I'll wear the dress out in fact. How much do I owe you?" I took out the wad of money Julien had left, which just covered the cost.

"Thank you, American lady," she said, her tone cutting.

I gave her half a smile as I took the bag and walked out, heading back to Gianna's, fuming by the time I got up there. If Julien wanted to fuck around, that was fine by me.

But I'd be damned if he was going to fuck me while he was at it. And without a condom.

"VERY NICE DRESS," GIANNA SAID WHEN I WALKED BACK INTO the café.

That made me smile and I smoothed my hands over the fabric. "Thanks. I also bought these." Gianna admired the two blouses I held up.

"Myra does good job," she said, checking the stitching on one of the blouses. "She makes everything herself."

"It wasn't Myra who helped me." I wanted to know about Angela. In fact, I couldn't not ask. "Angela was there."

Gianna's expression changed a little, her lips tightening as she exhaled as if she knew what I was trying to say and she wasn't surprised by it. "Angela is back for the season to help her old grandmother."

"She doesn't live here?"

"No, she lives in Rome."

"She told me she ran into Julien last night." I paid extra attention to folding the blouses in order to avoid Gianna's knowing gaze.

"She is a child. Twenty, barely." Gianna shook her head, dismissing her. She then put her hand on my arm so that I looked at her. "My grandson too clever to be distracted by such girls."

I nodded, wanting to end this conversation. A conversation I should never have started.

"What do you need me to do?" I asked, taking the apron she handed me and slipping it on while I looked around behind the counter.

I spent the afternoon making simple lunches and chatting with the customers who came into Gianna's café. There were several American tourists and I didn't realize until after talking to them how much I missed Americans, how much I missed hearing my own accent, talking to people who thought like me. I loved traveling, loved Italy specifically, but here, I was a foreigner, and it felt good to just have a casual conversation in my native tongue and know I was being understood.

Every time the door opened, I looked up, annoyed to find myself disappointed when it wasn't him. Finally, at a little after three in the afternoon, there he was, strolling in with freshly washed hair that was still wet, wearing a pair of jeans and a t-shirt. Even though I'd been watching for him for the last couple of hours, seeing him still made me jump, made my heartbeat pick up a little.

He walked in casually enough, but his gaze searched the café until he found me — and in that moment, I knew he'd been looking for me too.

"*Ciao*, Julien!" Gianna went to greet him while I stayed behind, still able to watch through the pass-through space between the kitchen and the bar.

"I was wondering where you were," he said to me when I was within earshot.

"I had to buy new clothes," I said, nodding to Gianna who took the plate and left us alone.

Julien grinned and I felt a sudden need to confront him about Angela — which was completely stupid.

"You had left me the note and the money." I didn't thank him. If he hadn't torn my things, I wouldn't have needed to buy anything.

"I expected you to be back at the house once you'd finished."

I shrugged my shoulder and turned to slice a piece of bread even though all the lunch orders had been filled. "I guess I don't read minds. Besides, it's not like you tell me who you're meeting at night," I added, flicking a glance at him before slicing the sharp knife through the bread.

Julien paused, then, when I heard him cluck his tongue, I set the knife down and turned to him, wiping my hands on the apron.

"Make me a sandwich," he said, his eyes narrowed a little, his lips in a much too comfortable smirk.

"Make your own sandwich," I said, untying the apron. "I'm on break."

I walked out of the kitchen then but when I passed the bar, he stood, grabbing hold of my hand and pushing me down hard onto the stool he had just vacated.

"Ouch." My butt still hurt when it made contact with anything, but he kept me there anyway, his eyes on me as he held me in place.

"If you're on break, you should sit," he said calmly, then smiled. "Remember what rude behavior gets you, Mia?"

Gianna walked behind the bar then and I wasn't sure if she hadn't watched the entire exchange. "You must eat, Mia. You are too skinny. I will make you both sandwiches you can take with you. I think the rush is over, Mia. Thank you for helping me."

Rush wasn't exactly how I'd have described the last few

hours. There had been customers, yes, but I still felt like Gianna was happy just having the company.

"You're welcome, Gianna. Maybe I can come back tomorrow if you'd like the help? I could use the *pleasant* company," I added, casting a sideways glance at Julien.

His grin widened and he gave me a wink. "Let's get those sandwiches and we'll go on a picnic. I didn't realize you were feeling lonely." He laid his hand over mine where it rested on the countertop.

Gianna mumbled something, but went behind the counter to work. Within a few minutes, Julien was escorting me out the door carrying a basket with a picnic blanket, sandwiches, two bottles of water, and a bottle of wine.

15

JULIEN

*S*omething was up with Mia, and when she grabbed the bag with her new clothes from Myra's, I had an idea what it was. If she'd gone into Myra's shop, chances were she'd met Angela. And I knew women like Angela. But to actually consider that Mia might be *jealous*?

Well, that was a whole other can of worms.

We walked in silence through the village, ducking into an alley where Charlie and I had found a path out into the surrounding countryside many, many years ago. I was glad to see it was still there, that same hole in the fence, even if it was overgrown with grass and weeds.

"Here," I said, pointing. I handed the basket to Mia while I climbed up, holding back a few of the branches and reaching out for the basket. She handed it to me and I set it down, then I offered her a hand.

"Where are we going?"

"Out here."

"Obviously. What is out there?"

I gestured for her to give me her hand. "A meadow where I used to come to when I was a kid."

She studied me for a moment and I wondered yet again why I bothered answering her questions, why I didn't just tell her to shut her mouth and get her ass up here.

Mia held on to my hand and I pulled her up the two steps. I then picked up the basket and walked the overgrown path. I still remembered it like it was yesterday. Familiar trees marked the way; a broken down, abandoned shed; stone fencing that had fallen apart centuries ago — all as if nothing had changed in the last twenty plus years.

"Charlie and I used to come here," I said, pausing to get my bearings before continuing. "Used to swim in the lake over the summer."

"There's a lake?"

"A little farther. It was huge to us back then. I wonder how big it will look now."

"Your grandmother said you'd gone to the cemetery."

If she felt me stiffen, she didn't say a word. "She has a big mouth."

"She's lonely. And you're right, she has some guilt."

I turned to her, pausing. "Are you two best friends now?"

"No, but I like her. And I can see she's trying to do the right thing."

Her green eyes stayed level with mine until I had to look away, tugging her behind me. "Too little, too late."

We walked in silence the rest of the way. It was another mile to the spot and when we came upon it, it was exactly as it used to be. I had to stop, a smile spreading over my face. This place was good. The memories were good.

"Wow, it's beautiful," Mia said.

I nodded. We were nearly to the top of the mountain. It was cool now, but in the summer, it was perfect. Charlie and

I would swim for hours here. We'd pack some food and spend whole days like this.

Red poppies dotted the lush, green grass and Mia followed me closer to the lake where I lay the blanket out and sat down on it, turning to her.

"Sit."

She did.

"The dress is nice."

She looked down at it. "Thanks. *Angela* helped me pick it out."

Her tone said it all.

"That's what this is about?" I asked.

"That's what what is about?"

I shook my head and leaned in close to her. "What did Angela say to you?"

"You mean did she tell me you were with her last night?"

I watched her face closely, her neck and cheeks reddening a little, her eyes darting every which way but toward my own.

"Mia." I took her chin in my hand and made her look at me. "What did she say?"

"She suggested you'd spent some time together with her and if you want to do that, that's fine. I mean, I'm not... we're not..." She pulled out of my grasp and picked at the grass, then turned to me. "How many women do you need to fuck in one night, anyway?"

I laughed. I couldn't help it. It was the way she looked — angry, but trying to act like she didn't give a shit.

"Screw you!" She tossed the handful of grass at me and got up, looking around as if for an escape.

"Sit down, Mia."

"Fuck you, Julien!"

With that, she turned and ran.

"Don't make me chase you." Really, where was she going to go? She'd get herself lost, if anything. "Mia! Come back here!"

She didn't even look over her shoulder. Instead, she ran toward the wooded area beyond which was a cliff.

"Christ." I got up and went after her. I could catch up with her easily, but I enjoyed the chase. Enjoyed listening to her trying to catch her breath, to find her way.

But she didn't tire as easily as I thought she might, and she led me in fucking circles for longer than I wanted.

"Mia!"

She snapped her head back to look at me.

"Don't make me come get you."

I'd have to punish this little show of defiance and my palm was itching to do it. Plus, I was hungry. I hadn't eaten since yesterday.

"Go away!"

"There's nowhere for me to go. Or for you, for that matter." She resumed her run and I followed, determined now to catch her. "There's a cliff, Mia," I called out from behind her. "I'll give you one chance to stop."

She didn't reply but picked up speed and at that, I did the same. This time, I caught up with her just as she neared the rocky ledge, the sudden drop surprising her. She tried to catch herself, but the grass was damp and slippery. I reached out a hand to catch her, gripping hold of the neck of her dress, hearing it tear just a little before I managed to grip her arm and drag her backward.

"Let me go!" she yelled.

"Let you go where?" I yelled back, dragging her to a fallen tree, bending her over it, holding her down with one hand while tugging her dress up with the other. "Over the fucking cliff?" I tugged her panties down while she struggled and as soon as her ass was bare, I smacked it hard. "Did you want me to let you go over the cliff, Mia?"

"Ow! Stop! You jerk!"

"You don't really get it, do you?" My cock was hard at the sight of her bent over like this with her panties down around her knees. The marks of the belt hadn't fully faded yet and her ass bounced beneath my hand, the red deepening after each slap.

"Stop, please!"

I gripped her hair and yanked her head backward so she looked at me while I slapped her ass again. She cried out, tears streaming down her face.

"Listen up, Mia," I said, tugging once more, landing one more spank before I gripped her ass. "This right here," I said, squeezing one cheek so she shut her eyes against the pain. "This ass belongs to me until you pay me that half million I'm more than earning here."

"More than earning—"

I smacked again, silencing her.

"When I tell you to sit, you fucking sit. You don't go on a fucking run through the forest to the edge of the cliff!" I moved my hand lower, gripping her pussy. "This here—"

"Please."

"This wet little cunt also belongs to me, just like this asshole does." My thumb pressed against her back hole, making her squeeze her eyes shut when I pushed in. "We could have had this conversation in a grown up manner, but you chose to act like a fucking child running away like that." I let go of her hair but kept my fingers inside her. "Stay down. Don't fucking move, or you're going to get more than a finger in your ass."

"I hate you."

"No, you don't. If you hated me, you wouldn't care who I fucked."

"I *don't* care who you fuck—" she snarled, squeezing her ass cheeks together when I tried to pull them apart, pushing my fingers deeper inside both holes.

"Soft. I want your ass cheeks soft. I'm going to watch my fingers disappear inside your cunt and your ass."

Her breathing pattern changed. It was coming fast and ragged, but there was more to it than fear. She was aroused. The wetness of her cunt already told me that.

"I've got your full attention now, don't I?"

She wouldn't open her eyes.

"Finish your sentence, Mia. Tell me that you don't care while I finger fuck you."

"I… I don't care who you fuck. I just care how many you're fucking while you're fucking me."

"First of all, I'd just like to clarify that we, and by we, I mean you and I, did not *fuck* last night. You sucked my cock and I ate your pussy. There's a difference. And I think you do care."

A moan she obviously tried to suppress slipped from her lips when I rubbed my fingers over her clit.

"I didn't fuck Angela," I said, pulling my finger out of her ass and unzipping my jeans. "Stay just like you are." I positioned myself behind her, gripping her ass with both hands and pulling her open, looking down at her pretty, glistening pussy, her dark little asshole. I'd fuck that soon too, but right now, I wanted that dripping cunt. "I didn't *touch* Angela in fact."

I thrust in to the hilt, her passage too tight at first, the noises she made sounding as good as her pussy felt squeezing my cock. "What I'm doing now though"—I pulled all the way out and thrust in again—"*that's* fucking. And while I'm fucking you or eating your pussy or anything else I choose to do, I promise to only do it to you. Better?"

But by then, she couldn't quite speak because I wrapped one hand around her hip and reached for her clit, rubbing the swollen nub.

"You feel good, Mia. Your cunt feels good and tight."

"Julien... I..."

"Come, Mia. *Fuck.* Come on my cock."

She called out as I said it, her walls contracting around me, squeezing, milking me as I came, thrusting hard one last time before I stilled, buried to the hilt, my cock throbbing as I released inside her, her juices squeezing out from around it.

I stayed inside her for a while, just feeling her, her warmth, her softness. She turned her face to watch me, her breathing still ragged.

I took off my t-shirt and wiped her clean before pulling her panties up and dropping her dress down to cover her ass.

Her legs trembled as she straightened and we walked quietly back to the meadow.

"Sit down."

This time when I said it, she obeyed and sat quietly. I joined her and reached into the bag to hand her a sandwich, which she took and began to slowly unwrap.

I twisted the corkscrew into the bottle of wine and popped it out, pouring a glass and inhaling. "My grandmother must like you. That, or she's hoping to get us drunk. This is the good stuff she bottles herself."

I handed it to Mia and she took it, inhaling and almost cracking a smile at my joke.

"You okay?" I asked. I didn't like hurting her. In fact, I saw something in her that was like the thing inside me that I tried to keep buried deep, down where it would never see the light of day. Where I'd never have to look at it. But to see it in someone else — no, to see it in *her* — that was different. And difficult.

Her eyes reddened and she looked down, picking at the bread on her sandwich. "Just... confused."

"About Angela?"

"No." She looked right at me then. "I want to hate you."

I watched her. God, she was so fucking different from anyone I knew, anyone I'd ever known. She was honest — and she was innocent.

And it scared the shit out of me.

"Just eat."

"I want to hate you, but I don't. And I think I understand you, in a way."

Now it was my turn to avoid her gaze, because if she kept looking me in the eye, she was going to see things I wasn't yet ready to face.

She shook her head, as if having a conversation with herself, and drank down the rest of her wine. I picked up the bottle and refilled both of our glasses.

"How cold was the lake when you used to swim in it?" she asked.

"Freezing." I laughed at the memory, how Charlie and I would dare each other to jump in.

She picked at her bread, but didn't eat a bite of it. "Jason raped me. I was thirteen. That's why the file was sealed. That million? Samuel paid my sister to shut her up, to send me away — and she did. They sent me off to the best boarding school money could buy and told me not to say a word, that no one would believe me. That it wouldn't be good for me. Wouldn't be smart."

"Your sister told you that?"

Fuck.

I knew the first part — it had to be something like that. But her sister's actions?

"No, that was Samuel. But my sister went along with it. She didn't intervene, didn't speak at all. She wouldn't even look at me. I'm not sure she could…"

Mia grew silent, absently making crumbs out of the bread in her hands. When she met my gaze, her eyes were red and when she brought her finger to her mouth to bite the nail, I saw how her hand trembled.

And when she tried to smile, to somehow make light of it, she fell apart.

I watched her for a minute. I just sat there like a fucking idiot watching her cry.

"Mia," I finally said, tentatively touching her shoulder.

She shook her head and pulled away, taking a handful of the napkins my grandmother had packed and wiping her face, her eyes, and her nose. I tried to pull her to me then, but she pushed me away and stood, sucking in a final, shaky breath and forcing herself to look at me.

"I'm tired. I'm just going to go back to the house, okay? You stay here. I know the way. I won't go anywhere else, I promise."

I stood, but when I reached out to touch her, she backed away.

"No. Just… please. I need to be alone."

I nodded. Like a coward, I nodded, and I watched her nod back and look around, lost, before quickly turning, and, without another word, disappearing back down the path.

16

MIA

I didn't tell him the half of it.

Jason's attacks began within a few weeks of him having come home for the summer. The rape wasn't a one-time thing. I'd been thirteen and he'd just turned eighteen. He should be rotting in jail for what he did to me, but instead, he somehow got out — and I was the one being punished for his sins.

I'd been so scared of him, so scared of what he'd do to me, to my sister, if I told. I wasn't even sure Samuel knew what his son was capable of. I wondered if he ever learned the truth of what happened to Tanya, now that she was dead. But when I found out I was pregnant at fourteen, everything changed.

When Julien had asked me if I was protected, I meant I couldn't have babies, not that I was on any sort of contraception.

It had taken me two weeks after taking the test to tell Jason. With what intention — given my limited options — I didn't like to think about right now. I didn't want to know what I was capable of. But he took care of things himself. I never even had the chance to make the decision. I'd barely finished my sentence when I'd felt a blow to my stomach so hard, I'd fallen to the floor, clutching my belly in agony. But he hadn't stopped there. He'd wanted to make sure it was done. That was how my sister had found out. When she'd come home to me bleeding in the bathroom, my stomach a landscape of purple and blue, the pain of my beating, of the resulting loss crippling.

"Mia."

It was Gianna calling from just outside the café door, but I only glanced at her before picking up speed in my attempt to reach the house before anyone else saw me. I'd kept this down for so long, kept all the hurt, the anger, the feelings of betrayal, and then guilt buried so deep inside me, that they were coming now and coming like a tidal wave.

No. Like a freaking tsunami.

I fumbled with the key at the door, but my hands shook so badly, that I dropped it twice. The third time I went to pick it up, Julien's shadow fell upon me. I looked up at him from my crouched position. He stood in jeans, shirtless, his face etched with worry, his breathing coming fast as if he'd been running. Without a word, he took the key, unlocked the door and lifted me to stand. He held me for a minute in the doorway, standing so close to me I could feel the heat coming off his body. He opened his mouth to say something, but then just rubbed both hands over my bare arms and turned me to walk inside. I did, and he closed the door behind us. As soon as it was closed, I tried to pull free to go upstairs, to hide under the covers in bed and sleep. Or at least hope for sleep. But he didn't let me go. Instead, he pulled me to him, one hand cradling my head, the other rubbing my back.

I wailed into his chest then. I wept like I hadn't been

able to at my sister's death. Like I hadn't ever mourned all of the losses since the day Jason St. Rose came into my life.

All the while, Julien held me.

He didn't speak, didn't try to comfort me. He simply held me, keeping me tight to him as I told the story, the whole of it. I'm not sure he understood a word between the sobbing, desperate sucking in of breath and letting loose of emotion, but he stayed with me. He listened. And when it was over, he lifted me up in his arms, my body going limp from the release, and carried me up the stairs where he lay me in the bed and pulled the covers up to my neck. He then closed the shutters to darken the room, and sat down beside me, petting my hair softly until I fell asleep, exhausted.

WHEN I WOKE, IT WAS TO THE SMELL OF SOMETHING delicious cooking. My stomach growled when I inhaled deeply and I turned to sit up, my head hurting a little. A glance at the clock on the nightstand told me it was nine o'clock at night. I'd slept the entire afternoon away, but I felt good. I felt lighter, my belly relaxed. I hadn't realized the tension I'd been holding was so heavy, but the stress of the last few days, on top of the running, the hiding, the mourning I'd been needing but unable to allow myself... it had all turned into this boiling cauldron of toxins.

And this afternoon, telling Julien, telling him everything — it had somehow become a sort of confession, a redemption.

The door opened then and Julien peeked his head inside the room. His gaze was cautious, and for a moment, I felt embarrassed at what had happened, at having let him see me like that, undone, raw.

I opened my mouth to speak but had to clear my throat when the words refused to come.

"I cooked," he said, leaning against the doorframe, looking a little unsure himself. "And it hasn't burned yet, so we should eat."

His eyes held questions in them, but he kept silent, watching me, waiting for me.

I smiled and pushed the blanket off. "I'm hungry. Ravenous, actually."

His smile widened. "Come, Mia."

I swung my legs off the bed, thinking how the last time he'd said those words, their meaning had been very different. My ears felt hot at the thought, but I lowered my gaze and made a point of making the bed before turning to him again.

Julien took my hand and led me down the stairs and to the kitchen where the large window was open and stars shone bright in the clear night. He'd set the table and pasta boiled in a pot on the stove.

"Sit down," he said, pouring a glass of red wine and setting it in front of me as I lowered myself into the wooden chair.

Unbelievably, I still felt tired. Tired, and weak.

Julien heaped two plates full of pasta and covered them with red sauce, then brought them over to the table and took a seat across from me. "*Buon appetito.*" He picked up his fork and spoon, rolled his pasta onto his fork and ate. "It's good," he said, nodding, smiling as if he were surprised.

I smiled back and picked up my fork and spoon, trying to roll it like he was doing but not doing it quite as well. His mouth still full, he set his utensils down and took mine.

"Like this." He rolled me a forkful and fed it to me.

"God, that is good."

He picked up his own fork and spoon and smiled proudly. "My great-grandmother's recipe. My grandmother still follows it to the letter. The woman can't cook otherwise."

"I just assumed all Italian grandmothers could cook."

"Well, you know what they say about assuming."

He smiled at me kindly, his eyes still searching, but cautious. We ate like that, having light conversation, being nicer to each other somehow. Something had changed between us this afternoon. It had probably been changing or evolving ever since that afternoon in my apartment, when he killed the men Jason had sent and taken me himself, keeping me safe, even if he himself hadn't come with the best of intentions.

"More wine?" he asked, his accent seeming stronger now that we were back in his village. He didn't wait for a reply before he poured for me and then emptied the last of it into his own glass.

Once I finished my plate, I sat back, content, and watched him watch me.

"Thank you," I said, the silence finally growing too awkward.

He cocked his head to the side. "You haven't told that to anyone, have you?"

I shook my head.

"Why did you tell me?"

"I have no idea." And I didn't want to discuss that really, so I got up and picked up the dishes. "I'll wash since you cooked."

Julien stood too and I noticed again how tall he was, how much space he took up in the small house. He'd put on a clean t-shirt since the afternoon, a crew neck that stretched tight across his muscled chest and arms. He took a step toward me and the dishes I held clattered as my hands suddenly trembled.

"Put them down."

He came closer and relieved me of the dishes when it seemed I was unable to do it alone. He then put his hands at my chest and pushed me backward so I leaned against the wall, his body pressing me to it, my face at his chest, my chin touching it when I looked up at him.

"Julien—"

"Mia." He snaked his hands up to my neck and entwined his fingers into my hair, tugging my head upward.

I licked my lips while he watched me, feeling the steel of his cock pressing against my belly. Without a word, he kissed me, tugging on my hair as he did, his kiss igniting a fire from the very center of my being, making my legs go weak. I opened my mouth to him, or my mouth simply opened to his, the command having been a silent one as his tongue slid into it. A low moan vibrated from his chest, and his grip in my hair grew harder as his other hand slid up my dress to cup my bottom.

"Who does this belong to?" he asked, his voice a whisper, his eyes on mine, their blue gaze darker with arousal.

"You," I managed, reaching for another kiss but unable to connect my mouth to his when he pulled my head back by my hair.

"Take your dress off before I tear it."

He gave me the tiniest space but kept that hand in my hair as I reached back to unzip the dress, letting me go only when I pulled it off over my head. He looked down at me, at my white lace bra and panties, new from this morning's shopping trip. Grabbing hold of my hips, he moved down to lick one nipple through the lace, the rough texture of the fabric mixing with the soft heat of his mouth, making my flesh harden, sending heat straight to my clit. His hands circled around to grip both my buttocks, squeezing.

He stepped back for one moment, only long enough to lift his shirt over his head and bare his chest to me. My hands wandered across the broad planes of his flesh, tracing the tattoos, feeling the strength of the man beneath.

I wanted him.

I wanted this man, this killer, the one who had now become my keeper.

He kissed me, pressing me against the wall, pushing the cups of my bra down beneath my breasts so that the hardened nipples scraped against the warm flesh of his chest. I reached to take his zipper down, taking hold of his cock, rubbing the slippery pre-cum over the length of it as he pushed my panties to the floor and lifted me, his cock against my belly.

"Who does this pussy belong to?" he asked, lining up his cock at the entrance and thrusting once, hard.

I grunted with the force of it. "You."

Both of his hands cupped my buttocks and I wrapped my legs around his hips, supported now between his body and the wall as he thrust into me again.

"And who does this ass belong to?" he asked, a finger pressing against my back hole.

"Ah... you." I wanted him. I wanted him like I'd never wanted anyone in my life. I could have come the way he was moving, his finger inside my ass, his cock in my pussy, his eyes glued to mine as if he were determined to watch every reaction, every little change in expression.

"You like being fucked, Mia?"

"By you." I kissed him, squeezing my cunt around his cock, making him groan.

"You like being my little slut?"

"Yes."

"You like my finger inside your ass?"

"God, yes. Please, Julien..."

But he pulled out then, an evil grin curving his lips while I desperately tried to climb back on top of him.

He shook his head. "Come," he said, taking my hand and grabbing the bottle of oil on the counter.

"Where—"

"I like it dirty, Mia. And I think you like it dirty too."

He sat down on the couch, the lamps on either side of it casting us in soft light. Setting the bottle down, he took hold of my wrist and looked up at me.

"I want to fuck your ass tonight."

My mouth fell open and I recalled the size of his cock. I pulled back a little, trying to free myself as I realized why he'd brought the oil over.

He grinned and pulled me down over his lap, holding me to him. My hands and feet went to the floor.

"No..."

"First time?" he asked, one hand pulling my bottom cheek out, the other taking the bottle of oil.

"You can't, Julien, it's... you're too big." I struggled but when he landed two quick smacks on my ass, I stopped and covered my bottom.

"That hurts!"

"Then don't make me spank you. Put your hands and feet down and push your bottom out to me. And answer my question. First time ass fucking?"

"Why do you have to be so crass?" I asked, craning my head back to look at him, catching his wolfish grin.

"Because I like it. You want to be spanked first?"

I shook my head.

"Then move your fucking hand. And answer my question."

"Can't you just—"

He smacked the side of my hip in response.

"Ow. Okay, just stop spanking me!"

I moved my hand and looked down at the floor, every part of me tense.

"Now, answer my question."

"You know the answer," I said to the floor.

"But I like to hear it. Last chance," he said, pulling my bottom cheek out again, the first dribbles of oil landing along the cleft between my cheeks.

"Yes."

He set the bottle down and kept one hand on one cheek, pulling it out, and with the other, began to smear the oil over my back hole. It felt good. God, it felt good, especially with his thigh beneath my clit.

"Push your ass out to me."

I did, hollowing my back, offering myself to him.

"We'll go slowly," he began, circling my asshole, before dripping more oil directly onto it feeling it slide down over my pussy, onto my thigh. "First one finger."

Instinctively, I tightened, and he *tsked* at me.

"No, Mia. I don't want to take what's not given. Relax, and open up for me. That's it. It feels good. You came with my finger in your ass more than once. You'll come again with my cock inside it tonight."

I moaned when he pushed his finger slowly in to the hilt.

"That's it, relax. My cock is getting hard for you, Mia, can you feel it?"

Could I feel it? Christ, it was stabbing my belly. I nodded

my head as he pulled his finger out, poured more oil onto the hole and went back in.

"That's it, relax. I'm going to fill this little hole with oil and make it nice and slippery for my cock."

God, I was going to come just from his words.

"Second finger now. Relax."

I tensed as quickly as he said it, but he just pulled my cheek out wider and pressed on, stretching my asshole with his fingers, his other hand coming around to rub my clit.

"That's it, just relax," he said, adding a third finger.

"Too much!" I tried to rise, but he pushed me back down.

"My cock is a lot bigger than my fingers, Mia. Take it."

I swallowed, trying to relax and somehow, he worked his third finger in.

"You see the mirror over there?" he asked.

I turned my head and glanced at the mirror that hung on one wall and nodded.

"When I fuck your ass, I'm going to have you on your hands and knees in front of it so I can watch your face as you take me deep. So I can watch your face as I fuck your tiny, little virgin asshole, as I come inside it. And then, when I'm done, I'm going to make you stay there while my cum drips out of you."

"I'm going to come, Julien." It was a combination of what he was doing and what he was saying that did it, and before I'd even finished my sentence, I came — hard. His fingers slid easily in and out of me then, those of his other hand rubbing my clit vigorously as I bucked upon his lap, my fingers curling into the rough carpet, my pussy dripping onto his hand, his wrist.

"No more. Please!" I begged him to stop, to pull his

fingers out of me, to let go of my clit — but he only laughed and picked up the oil again.

"All right," he said, taking his fingers out. "I think you're ready." He poured more oil over and into my bottom hole before slapping my hip once and helping me to rise. He then kicked the ottoman toward the mirror and pointed to it. "Hands and knees, Mia. Ass to me."

Slippery oil dripped down my thigh, embarrassing me as I walked to the ottoman and climbed onto my hands and knees, presenting my bottom to him, waiting for him.

"Spread your knees wider and hollow your back. I want to be able to see that sexy little hole from here." He spoke as he stripped off his jeans and underwear, his huge cock at attention. He then took a handful of oil and smeared it all over himself while I watched. "Mia," he said, raising his eyebrows and gesturing with his head for me to do as he'd said.

I spread my knees wider, canted my hips, opening myself to him — and waited.

Julien took his time, sitting back down on the couch directly behind me, massaging his length as he watched me.

"I love your ass," he said, finally rising. "You ready for me to fill it? Ready to take this?"

I looked at his cock as he knelt behind me, his big hands covering my bottom cheeks, pulling me wider. When I hadn't answered by the time he'd settled, he smacked my ass once. Not hard, but just to get my attention.

"Ow. Yes."

"Tell me. Say it, Mia."

He brought the head of his cock to my ass then, sliding one hand around to play with my clit.

I squeezed my eyes shut as his thick cock stretched my

bottom hole. It hurt, but it felt good too and with the oil, he slid in easily.

Julien slapped my ass again, forcing me to open my eyes. "Ready, Mia?"

I nodded, barely able to speak as he began to slide his length inside of me, his fingers still working my clit. "Fuck me, Julien. Fuck my ass."

"That's a good girl," he said, one hand in my hair, forcing me to look up into the mirror, to meet his gaze. "I want to see you take me. I want your eyes on me."

I swallowed, tensing a little when he pushed too far too fast, pain and pleasure mixing, mingling.

"Push against me, Mia. Take my cock inside your ass. Like that, almost there."

"It feels... it hurts, but feels... so good."

He smiled and thrust in the last few inches, causing me to gasp, taking me more than a moment to adjust, to stretch and open. He watched me all along, still behind me, inside me. And once I'd relaxed, he let go of my hair and gripped my hips with both hands.

"You want it hard, Mia?"

I nodded, my eyes nearly rolling to the back of my head as he began to move inside me slowly.

"You ready for me to fuck your ass now?"

"Yes... yes, please."

With that, he pulled all the way out. "Eyes on me or you'll be punished. Understand?"

I nodded, needing him to fuck me, afraid of the pain, but wanting it too, wanting to feel him take me there, to feel him come inside me.

Without another word, he began then, thrusting hard, making me cry out. He didn't pause, and he didn't slow. Instead, he kept his grip tight and fucked me, fucked my ass hard, the oil easing the tight passage, and just as I felt his cock throb and thicken even more, I came, the walls of my ass crushing his cock, calling a moan from deep inside his chest as he thrust twice more, hard. Then he stilled and we came together, the throbbing of his cock against my sensitive walls intensifying my pleasure as he shot his seed inside me. When I thought of what he had said, that he would make me stay just like this and watch while his cum dripped out of me, I cried out, the orgasm almost too much, the pure sensation too much.

Finally, breathlessly, he slid his cock from me, and I lowered myself onto my elbows before him, my face on the leather ottoman, my ass high in the air.

And he kept his word.

He made me stay just as I was and stood back, watching as my face burned when his seed slid out of me, dripping onto the leather, the submission inherent in the act seeming to please him immensely. He finally helped me up from my position and hugged me to him, pressing his lips to my forehead before resting his chin on to the top of my head. It was silent while he held me like this, and although there wasn't anywhere in the world I would have felt more safe, there was something else too.

Julien was thinking. I could feel it.

And somehow, I knew not to ask what it was that he was thinking.

17

JULIEN

I was going to kill Jason St. Rose. I decided it that night. I was going to murder the son of a bitch and I was going to do it slowly.

I didn't mention this to Mia and if she suspected, she didn't say a word to me.

Mia spent the next two days at my grandmother's café helping make sandwiches, but mostly keeping my grandmother company. Although it was mid-week and not busy, they both seemed to enjoy it and it gave me time to figure things out.

I'd been doing some research on the St. Rose family, Samuel St. Rose in particular. I'd have to find out if that missing ledger was truly in Mia's possession. Mia's sister's death had been investigated and ruled an accident too quickly for my liking. That could only happen when money — the likes of which Samuel St. Rose certainly had — changed hands. But he'd been in love with her, according to Mia. Would he have killed her? And why, if she had stolen so valuable a book? Especially before getting it back? Even if Samuel wasn't directly responsible for Mia's sister's death, I wasn't convinced it was an accident.

So, did Jason or Allison have anything to do with it?

The thought of Allison nagged at me. She was too squeaky clean — and no one was that clean. Ryan hadn't been able to dig up a thing about her, apart from the fact that Jason had been out to see her several times since his release from prison. Whenever I brought her up with Mia, she'd shut me down, so I'd given her an ultimatum.

She wasn't allowed to have contact with Allison until I said so.

She'd agreed, but she'd had little choice — and I'd be checking her call history whether she liked it or not.

Finished with my coffee, I stood and grabbed my jacket. This was all giving me a headache.

Walking out the door, I headed to the café to collect Mia. I needed to get out of here for a while, and I wouldn't leave her unprotected.

"*Ciao*, Julien." My grandmother greeted me as soon as I walked into the café. "She fits in here," she said as we both turned to look at Mia talking with one of the customers at the bar.

She did too.

I turned to Gianna. "Well, don't get used to it."

The hurt on her face was unmistakable, and though it took me a moment, I closed myself off from it, and walked away.

"Mia."

Fuck.

Why had I done that?

"Julien, I'm just—"

"Let's go."

She glanced at Gianna, but I kept my gaze fixed on her.

"I said, let's go."

"Go, Mia. It is okay," Gianna said, coming around and taking a cigarette out of the pack lying beneath the counter. Gianna's gaze locked upon me. I could feel it, but I refused to acknowledge it.

"I'm sorry," Mia began.

"Now, Mia."

"I'm coming!" I took her arm and walked her out of the café. "What is your problem? You really hurt her feelings, you know that?"

"Yeah, well she hurt more than my feelings."

I walked fast toward the car, not sure what the fuck I was doing, not sure why I was so angry at the old woman. It was past time to forgive, wasn't it?

Mia stopped on the street and tugged her arm free. "You know, Julien, people make mistakes — and time changes people."

"Let's go, Mia. Walk."

"No. Not until you listen." She dug her heels in, crossing her arms and standing there in the middle of the street. A few people stopped to stare.

I took two steps back toward her. "Fine. I'm listening."

"She loves you. I think you know that too."

Fuck. I don't need this.

"I think she's really sorry about everything, Julien. I know it would mean a lot to her if you could forgive her."

I looked at her, at Mia standing there in the sun, her dark hair up in a messy bun at the top of her head, her eyes full of compassion.

"It's not that easy."

"Why not?" she shrugged her shoulders. "You only have each other now, Julien. That's all that's left, right? It can be as easy, or as difficult as you choose to make it."

Being back here hadn't been a good idea after all. It brought up too much crap I did not want to deal with — and that crap weakened me. "I listened, okay? Can we go?"

She studied me, and for a moment, I knew she could see straight into my soul, straight into things I didn't want her to see, things I didn't want anyone to see.

But there was no escaping her gaze.

"I'll think about it. Can we go?"

"Okay." Mia slid her hand into mine and we walked slowly toward the car.

"Let your hair down."

She pulled the tie out and worked her fingers through the waist length, thick veil of dark hair while I watched.

"It's still wet."

I stood captivated. She had no idea how pretty she was, beautiful even. She wore pink lip-gloss and mascara, but otherwise, nothing else. She didn't need anything. Her skin was flawless, a smooth beige, with thick eyebrows along with long, dark lashes framing those clear, bright eyes.

"What? Is there something on my face?" She ran her hand over her mouth. "I was eating a piece of cake with some powdered sugar —okay, a *lot* of powdered sugar."

I chuckled and opened the car door, but pulled her to me first. "No, I just like looking at you." She smiled up at me, her face dimpling on the one side as she did, and I kissed those pretty, pouty lips of hers, tasting the cherry flavor of her gloss before tasting her. She opened to me easily, trust finally established between us. It was the strangest thing. This woman whom I'd intended to do harm to had become something so different in the last few days. We'd both told each other things neither of us had ever shared before. I couldn't say what had moved me to do that. It hadn't been a conscious thought, that was for sure.

And since the day she'd wept in my arms, I knew I couldn't let her go again. Ever.

"You make me crazy," I said, sliding her hand over my erection.

"Maybe we should just go back to the house," she said through a kiss.

I forced myself to pull back and looked down at her. "No, let's go. I want to show you something."

I knew where I wanted to take her. There was a village at the top of a hill that was pretty much abandoned. It made Pitigliano look like a hopping metropolis.

"How long did you know I was watching?" Mia asked about forty-five minutes into the drive. "At the hotel, I mean."

"From the first minute you opened the curtains."

"Why did she... who was she? The woman you—"

I glanced at her before accelerating into the curve of the road. "She was not a good person. That's all you need to know."

Mia's expression was so serious.

"And one more thing you should know. Not all my jobs come from where you'd think. You'd be surprised at who buys my services."

She shook her head and looked out the window. "I don't want to know, actually."

"I wasn't going to tell you, Mia. What do you know about a ledger your sister allegedly stole from Samuel?"

Her gaze suddenly snapped to mine. That first, quick reaction gave me pause. Was it guilt I saw in her eyes?

"A ledger?" she asked, her voice faltering.

I nodded. "The real books for the St. Rose's business, I'm guessing."

"I don't know anything about it."

Her answer was hurried. Too hurried. "No?"

"No." She looked out the window.

"I'll ask again. Do you know anything about the ledger? Look at me when you answer."

She looked... at a space just beyond my shoulder. "No, Julien. I don't know anything."

"Here we are," I said, parking the car alongside one other just outside of the village walls. Mia wasn't telling the truth, but for now, I had other plans. Taking her hand, I led her through the entrance of the village.

"Wow, this is amazing."

I smiled, but it was forced. It hadn't occurred to me that she knew anything about that book, but what if I was wrong? Her reaction to my question wasn't what I'd expected.

"Wow, there's really no one here."

"It's too far for most tourists, and the village itself only has the one café. Apart from the views, there's not much here," I said, tugging her toward a narrow alley. "No shopping for the masses."

"Wait, I want to see—"

"First this." I led her down and around the small road to the broken-down structure toward the end. There, we climbed over rubble and through a dusty, dark interior using the light from either end of the house as a guide.

"What is this?"

I stepped out into the field and pulled Mia along with me. The grass was almost waist high there and in just a few steps, we could see all of Tuscany spread out below us. It was breathtaking.

"Oh, wow."

"I'm glad the tourists haven't discovered this. This garden would be destroyed if they had."

She tried to pull away but I turned her to me instead, my mind still working through this turn of events, this new idea that she perhaps knew more than she let on. I wanted to push, to know the truth, but I knew it was better to bide my time. For now.

"Pretty blouse."

She looked down at it. "Thanks, it's one of—"

"Open it."

Her eyes widened but I could see from the way she licked her lips, she was aroused. Her gaze darted around me. "Here? What if someone sees?"

With a hand on the flat of her stomach, I pushed her backward against a tree and kissed her before whispering in her ear: "I don't care." And I didn't. "Open it, Mia."

She hesitated for a moment, but then her hands moved to undo the buttons and the blouse fell open to expose her pretty lace bra. My cock grew harder as I reached for the cups and tucked each one of them under her breasts. "Now, the skirt. Drop it — and your panties."

Her nervous glance once more passed over my shoulder, but she reached for her skirt and slid it down her thighs, the panties following. Then she stood in an open blouse, her breasts exposed from over the cups of her bra, naked from the waist down but for a pair of shoes.

My gaze ran the length of her and she gasped when I covered her mound with the palm of one hand, two fingers working through the neat patch of hair.

"I want this shaved. I want you bare for me."

She nodded shyly, her hands trying to cover her nakedness.

"No." I pulled her hands away and opened her blouse fully before studying her breasts, the dark, hardened nipples. Just beside her stood the thick stump of a tree that at one point had obviously been used as a chopping block. "Put your foot on that. I want to see your pussy."

"Julien, are you sure no one will come?"

"I already told you. I don't care if they do. I want to see your pussy, Mia."

Her throat worked as she swallowed and raised one leg up, glancing at me from beneath thick lashes. She was coquettish. Not as innocent as she led me to believe. There was a lust in her eyes that matched my own.

Squatting down before her, I pulled her pussy lips apart and blew a hot breath over the wet folds, making her grip my shoulders with a gasp.

"I want you to come on my face, Mia." It was all I said before gripping her hips harder and closing my mouth over her pussy, licking the length of her once, twice, before sucking her clit. I sucked softly at first, then, as she began to thrust against me, I drew out the hard little nub, biting on it a little, just enough to make her dig her nails into my shoulders as I thrust two fingers into her dripping cunt. When I did, she gripped me harder, her breath coming in short gasps as she muttered my name and came on my tongue, her wetness dripping down my chin, over my face, my fingers, and my hand.

Unzipping my jeans with one hand, I pulled her down on top of me. I lay in the grass on my back, gripping her hips to impale her upon my cock with one hard thrust. She gasped, even though she was ready — more than ready — the passage stretching easily to accommodate me, her slickness coupled with the pre-cum glistening on the head of my cock making her slippery. Closing her eyes, she planted her hands on my chest as I fucked her, bouncing her on my cock, listening to the sounds of our fucking, to the sounds of Mia as the walls of her pussy clamped down around my cock. She came again then, groaning, pressing her clit against my belly as I ground her hips into my own.

I was on the verge of coming, on the very edge of orgasm when I heard the sound of footsteps too hurried to be a mere tourist.

Mia gasped, not yet comprehending as I reached for the weapon in my jacket, which I'd discarded nearby. As soon as I got a handle on the thing and pushed Mia to the ground, rolling on top of her and forcing her head down, a shot rang out, just missing us. Mia screamed and I fired in the direction of the noise. A man's figure quickly disappeared back into the house and I shot again, this time hearing a grunt and knowing I'd hit my target.

"Stay!" I yelled as I stood, pulling my jeans up and following the shooter whose steps I could still hear. He got out fast and just as I turned onto the alley and aimed my weapon at his retreating form, a family of laughing tourists passing our secluded alley came to a halt as the running man nearly crashed into one of the women.

"Look at that, mama," the little boy said, pointing at me.

I shoved my weapon into the back of my jeans and watched as the man ran off. The family picked up on the fact that something wasn't right just as Mia came stumbling out from the house.

"Let's go," I said to her, gripping her arm as she handed me my jacket.

"Julien?"

"Are you hurt?" I looked her over as she shook her head.

"There was blood by the door, so you got him."

"Not a good enough shot if he was still moving."

The family remained watching us but we walked fast toward our car as the sound of tires screeching confirmed I'd be too late to catch up with the shooter.

"Who was it? How did they find us?"

I unlocked the car door and watched the dark vehicle speed away, leaving a screen of dust behind them as they took the curves too fast.

"Julien?"

It could have been anyone. Hell, it could have been for me. But as I looked at Mia, I knew they weren't. They'd found her again.

"Give me your phone and get in the car, Mia."

"What?"

I shoved her into the passenger seat and took her purse when she hesitated, rifling through it and finding her cell phone.

"Julien, what are you doing?"

Scrolling through her call history confirmed my suspicions and I gave her one dark look before slamming the door shut. She'd called Allison that morning and their conversation had lasted long enough that the call could have been traced. If that were the case, then they knew about the house in Pitigliano — and we were no longer safe there.

18

MIA

"*T*alk to me!"

Julien fumed, taking the curves at break-neck speed, scaring the crap out of me.

"I'm trying to think, Mia. Trying to figure out how to keep us alive — and you making calls I've asked you specifically not to make isn't helping!"

"I just called her to tell her I was okay and not to worry about me. That's all!"

"And coincidentally, this very afternoon, we get shot at in a random village?"

"It's not her. It can't be, Julien. She's like a sister to me."

"A sister — not blood related I might add — whose brother you sent to prison, and who stands to gain a substantial amount of money if you A: don't show up to claim your inheritance, or, B: turn up dead."

I shook my head, but stopped trying to defend Allison. She wasn't part of this, she couldn't be, but he wasn't ready to hear it.

"Maybe it's your line of work that has you thinking this way?"

The look in Julien's eyes when I said it made me wish I could reel those words right back in, turn back time and make them disappear.

"My line of work." He drove off the main road so fast that I would have fallen over on top of him if I weren't strapped in.

"I'm sorry, I didn't mean that."

He drove toward an abandoned house, so many of which were scattered along the countryside here. "What are you doing? Where are we going?"

He glanced at me as he slowed the car. There was no one around for miles and only a few cars passed along the single lane main road we'd just been on.

"What am I doing? My line of work," he said, his gaze cold, completely shut off from me.

My heart thundered in my chest when we came to a stop. He was going to punish me.

He got out first and went around to the trunk, taking out a black duffel bag. I watched in the side view mirror as he stalked toward me. He'd taken off his jacket leaving him in only a t-shirt and jeans, all rock-hard muscle covered in so many tattoos that more ink than skin remained. Tucked into the waistband of his jeans was the sleek black pistol he'd used so easily.

He opened my door and stood to the side. "Get out, Mia."

I shook my head, unsure if I was unable or unwilling to move. My hands trembled as I stared up at him. Hell, every part of me trembled. "Julien—"

"I said out. *Now*."

"I—"

Before I could finish my sentence, he'd reached inside to release my seatbelt and dragged me out.

I screamed, trying to dig my heels into the ground, but he ignored me. His grip on my arm hurt, but he was just too strong, and when he hauled me up over his shoulder, all I could do was pound on his back and twist every which way to get free even though I knew I wasn't getting free, not unless he chose to let me go.

With one hand holding me and the other gripping that bag, he kicked the car door shut and began the ascent up toward that abandoned house.

"Julien! Julien, what are you doing?"

But he wouldn't speak, and in his silence, I read my future.

"Please, Julien. I didn't mean what I said. I'm sorry, I just—"

"Quiet."

I nodded, even though he couldn't see me. Tears dropped to the ground while I bounced on his back as he carried me and that bag up the hill. It was hot, the sun bright, warm on my now exposed lower back, my blouse working loose in my struggles. Julien's body felt warm beneath mine, and being held this way served to remind me how powerless I was, how he was so fully in control.

Once we got to the house, he set me down but held on to me, stepping so close that his chest touched mine. If he was trying to intimidate me, it was working. It had already worked.

Julien's icy blue gaze searched my face, the raw anger not quite gone, but rather reined in, leashed tightly.

"You're going to do exactly as you're told. Understand?"

I nodded quickly, goose bumps rising all along my skin even in the heat of the afternoon sun. This version of Julien... I feared it, feared him. All the tenderness of the last few days was gone, and in its place was the man I'd met in my hotel room that first day, the one who'd fucked that waitress over the hood of the car while I'd watched, the one who seemed to take pleasure from my pain.

"Good." He nodded and turned me, his grip hurting my arm as he led me into the house.

We looked around the place, but each of us for a different purpose. The roof was gone for the most part so the sun lit up the space which had at one point been a large kitchen. A long counter built of bricks and covered with tile stood crumbling. Julien set his bag on it before turning to me.

"Still. Do not move. Do not run. If I have to chase you, what you've got coming will be ten times worse, understand?"

Could he see the anxiety that had my belly in knots, had me shivering and hugging my arms around myself as I tried to process what was happening, what was about to happen? If he did, he didn't care and I guessed my expression told him I'd stay put because he nodded once before turning to unzip the bag. But when he began to empty its contents, I couldn't stay. I couldn't do as I'd been told because my body went into survival mode and I ran. Without even thinking, I turned and ran. Where I was going, I had no idea. There was nowhere to go.

"Damn it! I told you to stay put!" he roared behind me as I pushed the door we'd entered through and stumbled out, getting all of two steps away before powerful hands gripped me, throwing me off balance, making me fall backward. He caught me, dragging me back inside all while I screamed and fought, knowing all along that my punishment would be worse but unable not to fight, even as Julien held me to him, gripping my wrists with one hand and taking a long length of rope out of the duffel bag.

"Julien, please," I started as he began to wrap the rope around and between my wrists. "Please, whatever you think you need to do, you don't. Please, Julien, I'm sorry, I just—"

He stopped altogether, taking a moment to look at me, his gaze burning right through me, making me wish he'd look anywhere else.

"I said *quiet*. Be. Fucking. Quiet. You'll have reason to scream shortly."

I shook my head violently then, pulling back from him even as he held my wrists and resumed winding the rope, binding me tightly as I tried in vain to free myself. He tossed the length of it over a wooden beam overhead once, then again, securing it before turning to me. He pulled on the rope, forcing my arms upward, stretching me to stand tall, not stopping until I stood on the tips of my toes. And when he was finally satisfied, he tossed the rope over the beam three more times before securing the end of it to a rusted iron ring along the far wall.

"Please," I mouthed, the word not even a whisper. But he ignored my plea and instead ran his gaze along the length of me before meeting my eyes again. "Don't hurt me. Please." I wept as I said it and without the slightest change in his expression, he gripped the blouse I wore and pulled, popping the buttons off, making me scream as he tore at it until it fell to the floor, a ruined, useless piece of cloth.

Tears streaked my face, but he didn't care. Instead, he slid his hand into the waistband of my skirt and tugged so hard that I bumped into his chest, the skirt ripping and falling to my feet, leaving me in only bra and panties, hanging by my wrists, the rope scratching my skin.

Julien walked around me slowly and I dared not turn.

"Please, please," I tried once more, and this time, instead of telling me to be quiet, he walked easily toward the bag and dug through it until he found what he was looking for: a roll of duct tape. I shook my head as he tore off a piece and came toward me. Gripping the back of my head hard, he slapped the tape over my mouth, and looked at me like that, hair stuck to my wet face, tears streaming from my eyes, my body trembling in fear.

We stood like that for a long time, or for what seemed like a long time even though it was probably mere moments, until he exhaled with a slight shake of his head and swept the hair off my face, gathering the length of it and braiding it so it lay across my shoulder. The tension lessened a little, but I had a feeling it was the calm before the storm. I wouldn't let myself be fooled by this momentary tenderness. Once he'd finished braiding my hair, he put his hands on my shoulders and his eyes met mine again.

"I'm going to punish you first, Mia. I'm going to whip you for disobeying me and once we're finished, I hope you'll never make me repeat the lesson."

I shook my head, fresh tears beginning to flow. Although he stood in front of me, he ignored my pleas, which came like moans from behind the tape, and instead, reached behind me to undo my bra. He then took the knife from inside its holster on his belt and opened it, making a point of letting me see the sharp blade before he cut through the straps, ruining another bra, letting the lace drop to the floor before tucking the switchblade back into its holster.

He backed away just half a step to look down at me, his gaze hovering at my breasts, my nipples hardening under his scrutiny. Somehow, even through fear, my body was reacting to him the way it had learned to react to him. It was wrong and I knew what was coming would be pain, but my body and my mind were two wholly separate entities.

"Pretty," he said.

I glanced down when he stepped back and saw the rod of his erection pressed against his jeans. The thought that he was aroused should have made me sick, should have made me hate him, and even though I might just hate him once he was through with me, I didn't now. Somehow, the thought of it, of me so wholly within his control, powerless and bound, it made me shudder with desire.

And he saw it.

I knew it as soon as he looked at me and one corner of his mouth turned upward.

"Mia," he said, his eyes holding mine captive as he brought the flat of one hand to my belly and slid it down into my panties, thick, calloused fingers threading through the hair there before curving down, spreading me open and finding the evidence of my arousal.

And upon finding it, his grin widened and his eyes narrowed. He knew, and that knowledge crushed me.

I made a sound and closed my eyes when his fingers stroked my clit before dipping inside me. He stepped closer, closing the space between us so that his bare chest touched my bare chest. I turned my gaze up to his, one last plea in my eyes, but a plea for what, I could not say. Julien pulled my head into his chest then and withdrew his hand from inside my panties, wiping my wetness on my waist as he held me to him and kissed the top of my head.

"First, your punishment," he said, his breath at my ear. "A whipping you'll not soon forget." As he said it, I felt the cool leather of the whip I'd seen earlier at my thigh and all I could do was close my eyes and lean my forehead into his chest, my breath coming in short pants.

"Then, on my quest for the truth, an ass fucking — but not like the other night."

His free hand moved down my back and over my hip to grip one cheek hard.

"No, this one will be punishment. And if you're good"—the hand with the whip moved up toward my cheek, making me look up at him—"if you're very, very good, maybe I'll let you come while my seed seeps out of your tight little ass."

I trembled — desire, fear, panic, passion all warring within me, the sensations confused, thoughts muddled. And in his eyes, I saw that he saw.

"You know what gets me off, Mia?" he asked, stepping back.

Panic dominated as he unfurled the long whip and circled around me once.

"Looking at you like this."

I shuddered when the leather touched me, mewling from behind my gag.

"Bound. At my mercy," he said, one knuckle wiping at a tear. "Afraid."

He brought his mouth to my face and licked the tears that now slid down my cheeks.

"I can smell it, taste it." He looked at me. "Sick, isn't it?" he whispered, just biting my ear softly. "That I'll get off on your pain."

I swallowed. It was sick, or it should have been. And while I wept in anticipation, in utter terror of what was to come, when he pushed my panties down over my hips, I was wet. Even as he stripped me of that final barrier between us, preparing me for the lash, I was wet.

"Punishment," he said.

First, there was the sound of the cracking of the whip. It took me a split second to understand what had caused that crack, that it was leather colliding with vulnerable flesh — my flesh. As for the sensation? Fire. A line of pure fire burned across my ass just after contact, just after my mind processed that I'd been struck.

I bounced forward on tiptoe, trying to keep contact with the ground but supported by my restraints as I screamed from behind my tape-gag. Julien walked around me and I shook my head, pleading with my eyes. He took a step back.

"Look at me, Mia."

I did, and when I did, he struck the fronts of my thighs making me scream from behind the tape again, my eyes squeezing shut while my body processed the pain.

I looked down when he moved again, looked at the thin red line, wondering how he'd not broken skin. But before I could think, he struck again, this time along the backs of my calves once, then again just behind my knees.

I wailed, hopping up and down, trying to dodge the next stroke I knew was coming, but failing entirely when he lashed me across the tops of my shoulders then crisscrossed that stroke with another long ways down my back.

He came to stand in front of me, watching me, giving me time to breathe, waiting for me to calm, to look at him, and when I did, what I saw in his eyes, in the shadowy depths of those angelic, fierce blues, was a darkness that terrified me.

This man was danger. This man — he brought death.

And I wanted him, even now as he lashed me, God help me, I *wanted* him.

It was as if he was waiting for me to see, waiting for me to face my own strange desire before he continued, and when he did, he didn't taunt or tease. He did not walk around me. He did not give me time to catch my breath. Instead, he whipped me. He lashed me — my back, my buttocks and thighs, my calves, and the soles of my feet as I stood on tiptoe. The sound of the whip, that crack once heard never again forgotten, once felt, forever feared, burned into memory. And somewhere in the midst of this punishment I thought would kill me, I found peace, a quiet I did not expect, where all that was left was that cracking of leather against flesh, the burning aftermath of its passage, the pain.

"Three more," he said, the sound of his voice startling me.

It took me a moment to see him, to focus my eyes on him as he stood waiting before me.

He raised his arm and struck across the fronts of my thighs, a second line to match the first he'd left at the start of this. The next stroke, a softer one, cut across my belly making me double over, or at least try to, gasping.

"Last one." His eyes had darkened, the pupils dilated. He almost smiled, but when he delivered the final stroke with a simple flick of his wrist, the whip lashed me across my breasts, catching both of my nipples, making me suck in breath and grip the rope that bound me.

That stroke, that final one, changed everything. My body was a pure, throbbing agony, and from that pain, something else, something as hot as lava, bubbled at my very core.

The whip fell to the floor then, and Julien came to me, tearing the tape from my mouth before I was ready, the pain of it adding to the sting, the fire that consumed me whole. He crushed his mouth over mine, his tongue delving deep inside me as he pressed his body against me, his cock at my belly, the material of his jeans aggravating the too fresh lashes that I knew what fire was. Even while I wept, my thighs were wet with desire, and I kissed him back, wanting him, needing him.

After all that, I wanted him to take me. I needed him to possess and own me.

"Julien."

He undid his jeans and pushed them and his underwear to the floor, gripping the base of his thick, hard cock in his hand, rubbing its length, turning a slow circle around me.

He groaned behind me and I heard the sound of his breath coming faster. "Seeing you like this gets me off, Mia," he said, walking back around and untying the rope from the ring he'd fastened it to before coming to stand before me.

I swallowed, my heart racing as he loosened my bonds until I stood on flat feet once more. He looked at me and I brought my hands to his chest, unsure what he'd do next, if he'd make good on his promise.

I should have known he would.

His expression unchanging, he pushed me down to my knees, his hand gripping my hair. "Open your mouth," he said, his other hand at the base of his cock. "Spit on my cock, Mia. Then spread it all around. It's the only lubrication you'll be getting so make it good."

I opened my mouth and licked the tip of his cock, but when I tried to take him into my mouth, he pulled my head back.

"Spit on it."

He held his cock so it just touched my lips.

"And look at me while you do it."

How I was so aroused I couldn't explain, but as I knelt before him, my punished flesh still burning, my humiliation only beginning, I *was* aroused to the point that my thighs merely rubbing against my clit could have gotten me off. I couldn't deny it.

Keeping my eyes on his, I dribbled spit onto his cock, and he nodded his approval. "More."

I obeyed.

"Now, smear it around with your tongue."

I did, tasting him, tasting the salty pre-cum mixed with

my spit, licking the length of him until his cock glistened, and, satisfied, he pushed me farther down so I was on all fours before him. My hands still bound, rope splayed before me. I waited like that while he walked behind me, kicking my legs so I opened them wider and arched my back, some part of me getting something from this acquiescence, this yielding of my body to him, to his will.

Julien knelt between my legs then and gripped my hips.

"Down on your forearms. Face down too. Lift your ass up to me. Good, like that."

His fingers were first. He dipped them into my pussy and smeared that juice upward toward my ass and pressed until my body yielded, plunging his fingers inside me, stretching me.

My body fought it, fought him, but I remained in position and would. It was my penance, after all. I would atone.

He groaned and before I was ready, and with his fingers still inside me, I felt him line the head of his cock up to my ass. Panic struck again as he pushed, removing his fingers when my hole stretched to take him.

"Please, Julien. It's going to hurt." Weakness and fear spoke for me but he gripped my hips tighter when I tried to pull away.

"This is happening, Mia. Take it."

Perhaps he took pity on me then, or at least I thought so when he brought the fingers of one hand around to my clit and began to rub.

"Tell me about the book," he said, rubbing my clit, using my arousal against me as he pushed in a little deeper, stretching me wider.

"It hurts."

He moaned when I said it, as if pleased. He thrust once

more, not deep, but enough to make me gasp. "Time for truth, Mia. Push, and tell me about the book."

"Book?" Why was he talking about that now?

"The ledger. Where is it?"

He stopped rubbing my clit and thrust, taking another inch too fast, making me burn on the inside just as he'd made me burn on the outside with his whip. But just when it was too much, he resumed manipulating my clit with his fingers and my mouth opened as pleasure mixed with the pain, confusing me again, confusing my body, my mind.

"Ledger," he said again.

I nodded, looking over my shoulder. "I have it."

He smiled and leaned down to kiss my shoulder.

"Good girl." He thrust deeper. "Where is it?"

God, I was going to come if he kept moving like that, if he kept rubbing my clit like that. The sensation of having my ass filled like this, with his too big cock, his breath on me, his eyes watching as they extracted from me what they wanted, punishing me, pleasuring me, it was too much.

"I'm going to come."

He shook his head, and, bringing both hands to either side of my pussy, pulled my lips apart so nothing touched my clit as he claimed another inch.

"Not until you tell me — and then not until you're taking a proper ass fucking."

I nodded. Did I want him to stop? Did I want him to make me come?

I didn't have to answer those questions as he pushed again, claiming more of my ass.

I groaned and he shook his head. "Dirty girl," he said, his thumb back on my clit. "Tell me where it is so I can fuck you, and you can come."

I nodded again — it seemed it was all I could do — and

instead of waiting, he thrust inside of me one final time, the passage so tight he had to force the last of it. I cried out, but he stilled inside me, and this time, bit my shoulder lightly.

When he spoke, it was a deep timbre I felt as much as I heard. "I'm all the way inside you now, Mia. I can make this good for you or I can make it hurt. I don't mind either way. The ledger. Where is it? Last time I'm asking."

He withdrew slowly, readying to make good on his promise.

I had to tell him. I had no choice. But it wasn't only that. He could help me. He was already helping me. For a price, yes, but there was more between us, wasn't there?

Fool.

No, I couldn't listen to that voice. All of the events of the last days played like a movie in my mind, and I knew I had to tell him.

"At the train station."

He smiled and moved a little in and out, in and out, still ready to punish me unless I did what he wanted. "Good girl. Go on."

"In Rome. I put it in a locker when I took the train to Cosenza. It was all I could think to do with it."

"The key to the locker?"

"In my purse."

He looked at me, studying me as if to see if I were lying. "Look at me."

I did. I already was, but his face had grown much more serious.

"If you're lying to me, I will take the whip to you until you bleed. Understand?"

"I'm not lying. I swear."

His gaze narrowed for a moment, then his lips quirked

with a half smile. "Good. Now face forward and take your ass fucking like a good girl."

I did as he said as he pulled all the way out and thrust into me hard.

"Ah... Julien..."

"You're so fucking tight," he said through clenched teeth, fucking me harder, pushing my head down so my face lay on the ground. "This asshole belongs to me. As well as that pussy, and that mouth."

"Julien," it came as a gasp. He fucked me harder, faster, all while his fingers rubbed my clit, taking me to the very edge.

"When you misbehave, I'll punish all three of them. Understand?"

I nodded fast, biting my lip. I was going to come.

"But if you're good, I'll make you scream my name."

"Julien!"

He rammed into me then and didn't stop, sweat dripping from his forehead onto my back, all those parts of me where the lash had struck burning with a different sort of fire now, intensifying the pleasure, the pain merging with the orgasm that took me, took us both. When he stilled after one final, hard thrust and I felt him shudder and release inside me, I came, the world disappearing around me. It was raw bliss, utter and complete, nothing but sensation.

Once he'd finished, once I'd milked every last bit of his essence from that thick cock, Julien pulled out of me, making me look back at him as he kept me in position. His gaze held mine then moved to my throbbing, stretched ass as he watched his seed spill out of me, the humiliation of it somehow completing this scene between us, this punishment that had come out of anger... and turned into so much more.

19

JULIEN

*I*t was over.

Wrapping Mia in a blanket I kept in the car, I sat with her on my lap for a long time inside that broken down house just watching the sky darken, seeing the stars revealed, listening to her breathing when she finally slept.

After her punishment, I'd cleaned her, checking every one of the stripes that crisscrossed her body. I'd not broken skin — and it hadn't been my intention to do so. Although the whipping was a harsh punishment, I'd not struck as hard as I could have. I knew that once I'd begun concentrating the strokes at her back, that pain would evolve, transform. There was still pain — that was unavoidable, and the point of punishment — but she found some peace in it. I could see it in the way her body took the lashes, in the look in her eyes.

And beyond that, she'd grown even more aroused.

I wondered if I could perhaps train her to always link pleasure with pain, and pain with pleasure.

But that was for another time.

My cell phone buzzed in my pocket just as I was about to

wake her. I pulled it out and checked the display. It was Cash.

Mia groaned and moved a little, waking up slowly.

"Cash," I answered.

"Got your next job lined up," he said. I guess Cash could be called a sort of broker. Well, if you could have such a thing as a broker in my line of work.

"Oh yeah?" I looked down at Mia who was now looking up at me, listening, and at that moment, I wasn't sure I wanted another job.

"It's a good one. Hell, you don't even have to exterminate this one. Delivery only."

"Really?" That was curious.

"I'm sending the file now. Check your e-mail in a few minutes."

"Timeline? I'm a little... tied up." I moved my lips into a smile, tucking Mia closer.

"Then get untied. It's a lot of money."

"All right. Send the file."

"Just hit send."

With that, Cash ended the call.

"Who was that?"

I tucked the phone back into my pocket. "Colleague."

"You have *colleagues?*"

"I guess that sounds cryptic."

She shrugged her shoulder, then grimaced as she moved. Her cheeks flushed red and she lowered her lashes over her eyes.

"Why didn't you tell me about the ledger earlier?"

"We didn't exactly meet in a way that made me trust you."

"No, I guess not. Tell me how this story plays out."

"That money my sister left me, Samuel gave it to her to

make sure she kept quiet about the rape. I guess it was also to make sure I kept quiet. If I don't claim it, it goes back to them. I don't even really care about the money, I mean, a million is a lot—"

"Half a million."

"Still, a lot of money. But if Jason would leave me alone, just let me live my life, I wouldn't care about it."

"But you know he won't?"

"No, he won't. He's sworn it and he's vengeful." She studied me for a minute, the look in her eyes heavy. "I wasn't the only one he hurt."

It was my turn to study her.

"My sister. I don't know if Samuel knows."

"How do *you* know?"

"The note she left me, and something Jason said, the thing he said that made me decide. The night she died, she was leaving. She was running away. Maybe Samuel couldn't protect her from Jason? I don't know. Samuel loved her and she trusted him. Or she used to. She wouldn't have stolen from him. I kind of wonder if the book was my sister's way of giving me some insurance, you know what I mean?"

"Do you believe your sister's death was an accident, Mia?"

"It's too terrible to think otherwise, Julien. I can't do that."

"And it was after that that you went to the police?"

She nodded. "Maybe telling the police what he'd done to me was stupid, maybe I should have just kept my mouth shut, but I was scared. I had no money, no job, no college degree and at the memorial service for Tanya, he made this comment, this gross suggestion..."

"Hinting he'd hurt Tanya."

She nodded. "And that it was my fault. But with her out

of the way, I was alone. He made sure I knew that. Those years I wouldn't talk to her"—she shook her head, looking down—"can't get those back, you know?" She looked at me with the saddest eyes I'd ever seen.

"I know."

"But maybe I should have kept my mouth shut and run away, not been so stubborn, so hell bent on making sure he got what he deserved. My sister couldn't make him pay, but I still could. There is no statute of limitations for raping a minor."

"You did the right thing. The courageous thing. He raped and beat you to the point you miscarried. To the point you can't have children. Is that certain, by the way?"

She nodded, despair shadowing her eyes. "The doctor said it would be a miracle if I ever conceived, given the damage."

I nodded.

"He deserves to still be rotting in prison, Mia. You didn't do anything wrong."

"I know that. I just wish I wasn't in this whole heap of trouble. What do we do now? Are you still going to help me?"

"I'm not sure you'd survive if I didn't. Plus, half a million dollars." As soon as I spoke that last part out loud, I knew I was lying. To her. To myself. This wasn't about money for me. Not anymore. But I didn't have time to think about that yet. "You wanted to know what happens now? We get that ledger back and we get you the money you're owed — and disappear. Same plan, just expanded."

She smiled a little.

"Ready to go? We'll stop at the house to pick up some things and tell my grandmother we're leaving. I want her to be aware, just in case."

"You don't think anyone would hurt her, do you?"

"I can't see how they would have linked you to me, and without that, they wouldn't know who she was. Let's go. Can you stand?"

"Why did you do it? Why did you punish me like that?"

"I told you the answer to that the last time. I like to. Remember?"

She flushed red. "I... you didn't need to punish me at all."

At that, I chuckled and hauled her upright, gripping her ass cheeks hard. "As long as you're in my protection, you're mine to do with as I please. Punishment is part of that. Keep that in mind."

"I'm sorry I didn't tell you about calling Allison."

"As long as you understand you're not to have contact with her again, it's good between us." I inclined my head. "You paid the price. Or your back and your ass did."

She dropped her head down and the red on her neck and cheeks intensified as she nodded.

"Let's go. We've got a long night ahead of us."

First thing was first. We drove to Pitigliano. I wasn't sure what I was going to tell my grandmother. It was unlikely anyone would hurt her, but I didn't feel right just leaving her defenseless. Once I checked that the house was secure, I left Mia to pack up our few things and went to the café.

"Julien," she greeted me while stubbing her cigarette out.

"You should stop smoking, Gianna. It's bad for you."

Almost as bad as knowing me.

"And for you." Even though she chuckled, her expression was expectant.

I sat at the counter while she made an espresso. "We have to go. Mia and I."

She frowned. "So soon? Why?"

"She's in trouble and that trouble caught up with us this afternoon."

She put the small cup of espresso in front of me but didn't speak, just kept her eyes on mine. I reached into my pocket for my revolver, but as soon as she saw it, she shook her head no.

"Gran." It was what I used to call her when I was little. It had been a long time since I'd called her that.

"Put that away. What sort of trouble?"

"Bad sort. I don't want anyone to have linked you to this somehow."

She studied me. "I'm sorry I couldn't take you and Charlie, Julien. I'm sorry I couldn't be there when you needed me. I regret that still. Daily." Her eyes moistened but she didn't cry, just waited for me to respond to her confession. It was probably the first time she'd said that out loud.

I looked at this old woman in front of me, this aged version of my mother — even though I didn't really remember what my mom looked like anymore. It was the eyes. They were the same.

"Past is past," I said, meaning it, knowing I'd forgiven her even if it wasn't a conscious thing. In a way, realizing that, knowing that I'd forgiven her, I'd also forgiven myself — at least a little.

Mia walked into the café then. The girl just couldn't seem to listen, couldn't do as she was told.

"I have everything," she said.

"You were supposed to stay put."

"I wanted to say goodbye to your grandmother." Gianna came around the counter and hugged her while I took the bags out of Mia's hands.

"Will you be back?" Gran asked once I stood, ready to go.

"I hope so," Mia said, before I could answer — and I realized then how close they'd grown over the short time we'd been here.

"If anyone comes, Gran—"

"I may be old, but I can take care of myself, Julien. Don't worry about me. "

One of the old men who always seemed to be at the café stood up. "Your grandmother is safe. If anyone wanted to harm her, they'd have to deal with me first."

"And me," another man added.

I smiled at the crew of them, the two old men and my grandmother, and I believed them. They may have looked past their prime, but I had a feeling they could indeed hold their own.

"Take care of Mia. And Mia, you take care of my grandson. He's all the family I've got left. I expect to see both of you back here soon."

"We have to go. Gran. You have my phone number. Call me with anything. Understand? Anything at all."

She nodded and for the first time since I had been a kid, I hugged my grandmother again. She felt small, but strong, and I squeezed her tighter. "I'll see you again, Gran."

"Promise it." She sniffled at my shoulder and I patted her back.

"I promise."

When we pulled back, she quickly ran the back of her hand over her eyes, then gave Mia one more hug. "Take care of each other."

"We have to go."

"Good bye, Gianna," Mia said as I pulled her along. I looked back once more just before we walked out the door.

I'd made a promise, and I intended to keep that promise.

"I just have to check one thing. Get settled, Mia." After loading the bags, I retrieved my phone and opened the email from Cash. It contained the usual, a coded file to which only he and I knew the password. The file downloaded slowly, the text appearing first before any photos, and my chest tightened as I read the message.

The amount was one million dollars for delivery. Alive was preferable, but they would take dead — for a lesser payment, of course. But dead was only once she'd disclosed the location of a certain book. A telephone number and the delivery address were listed, along with the name of the buyer.

I felt like I was going to vomit.

The target's name was listed next along with birthdate and last known whereabouts. I closed the trunk as the photograph slowly loaded, almost pixel by pixel, and there she was, the photograph of Mia taken before I knew her. I looked at it, looked at her smiling face, then looked at the back of her head as she settled in before she turned to me and smiled.

I smiled back and pushed my phone into my pocket, making my way to the driver's side.

"Ready, Mia?"

She nodded. "You called her Gran," she said as I backed the car out.

"I did."

She squeezed my arm. "I'm glad."

꧁꧂

WE DROVE UNTIL MIDNIGHT THEN TOOK A HOTEL ALONG THE highway. I know Mia noticed the change in my mood, but she didn't ask about it. After a quick bite to eat, we went up to our room.

"So do you think we can just disappear? I mean, what are we going to do if Jason is—"

I gathered her up in my arms, loosening the embrace when she flinched. Her back would still be sore and I wasn't in the mood to talk about Jason. Not yet.

"Come here, let me have a look at you." I kissed her as I said it, my cock already standing at attention at the thought of having her naked soon. The intention was to distract her as much as it was to be close to her again.

One million dollars. One million to deliver her to her stepfather. It doubled the payment she offered me.

"Tell me something. Did you tell Allison about our deal this morning?"

"Am I in trouble again?" she asked, stiffening.

"No, I already told you we're clear. I just want to know what you told her."

"I told her you were helping me. I told her how I ran into you the day Jason's men had come and why you were helping me. Why I couldn't call her again until everything was settled."

And I guessed Allison had passed that message on to her brother or father, or both, who would know about the murdered woman at the hotel across from Mia's hotel room, the one Jason had sent his goons to. I wondered if father and son were working together now, but it didn't matter. What mattered was that if they contacted Cash, they knew about me. I didn't believe in coincidences like this one.

"Julien?" Mia said, looking nervous.

I shook my head, shrugging off the thoughts. There was

time for that, but not now. Now was time for something else. Looking down at her, I saw how small she was, how vulnerable. Without another word, I pulled her to me, one hand at the back of her head, the other on her hip. I crushed my mouth onto hers, my hard cock pressing against her soft belly while she opened for my tongue.

"I'm running out of clothes," she mumbled through my kiss when I pulled her blouse out of her jeans.

"I will take care," I said, smiling a little. "Although naked is always nice with you."

Breaking our kiss, I pulled her top off. She wasn't wearing a bra, but her breasts were small enough that she didn't need to, and I imagined the straps would have cut into her shoulders and back. Kissing her again, I undid her jeans and pushed them off as she worked my t-shirt over my head. Placing my weapon on the nightstand, I helped Mia step out of her jeans so she stood naked but for a pair of lacy white panties.

Sitting on the bed, I grabbed her wrists to stop her when she began to push them down. I held her like that and looked at her, at the faint pink lines of the whip, at her otherwise flawless skin. When she tried to pull free to shrug out of her panties, I stopped her and shook my head.

"Turn around."

She hesitated, but I insisted, nudging her to do as she was told. She turned and stood with her back to me, most of her skin marked, lined with soft pink strokes of the whip.

"Put your hands at the back of your head."

She craned her neck to look over her shoulder, barely able to meet my gaze. "Julien."

"Do as you're told, Mia. Look straight ahead and put your hands at the back of your head."

I saw her tremble as she slowly obeyed and I met her gaze in the mirror across the room.

Rising to my feet, I gathered up her hair and twisted it so she could hold it up off her neck and I kissed her shoulder, kissed the topmost stroke. I looked at her as I did it, watching her mouth open slightly as she shuddered while I kissed each of the strokes along her shoulders, her back, moving down her body as I did, sitting down behind her while sliding fingers into her panties on either side to draw them down over her hips and to her ankles. I kissed the lines on her bottom and her thighs before taking my attention to her naked ass.

"Widen your stance a little to shoulder width."

She did, the scent of her arousal one I'd come to know, one that made me salivate like a fucking dog.

"Now bend over and touch your toes."

She shook her head and broke position, covering herself as she faced me. "I can't... I—"

I stood and watched her lean backward when I covered the space between us, knowing the effect the difference in height between us had on her.

"Is your cunt wet, Mia?"

She looked down.

"I can smell it. Is it wet? Is it wet for me?"

She nodded, but wouldn't look at me.

"I thought so. I want you to show me that cunt now. You've done it before. You've shown me your cunt and your asshole. Remember? That first night?"

Her face flushed red when she turned wide eyes up to me ever so briefly.

"Now I want you to get back into position, turn your ass to me and bend over while I try to decide if I should come in your pussy"—I gripped her mound to a surprised gasp from her—"or on these pretty little tits." Smearing her juices on her belly, I dragged my fingers up to pinch one nipple. "Or"—I went farther up toward her mouth, her face—"or perhaps on your face after I fuck your mouth."

She swallowed, the scent of her filling the room now, and I sat back down.

"Ass to me, Mia. Let's go."

Although hesitant, she walked back toward me and turned to stand once more with her back to me.

"Good girl. Any preference as to where I come tonight?" I asked, just touching her back to encourage her to bend over. She moved slowly down, her ass spreading open as she did until she touched her toes. "God, that's fucking beautiful, Mia."

I heard her swallow and stood for a moment to relieve myself of my jeans and underwear so I sat naked on the bed, my cock a steel rod. "Arch your back, Mia. Push your ass out to me."

She did without hesitation now. I looked at her exposed like that, her pussy lips open, glistening between her cheeks, her asshole just visible.

"Tell me, Mia, where should I come?" I asked, standing to bring my cock to her pussy, dipping it into the tight, wet passage. It took all I had not to just fuck her, but I wanted more. "I won't fuck your ass tonight, although I do so enjoy that." I pulled my cock out, kneeling behind her so that my face was at the level of her ass. With my hands on her cheeks, I spread her wider and began to lick the length of her, more teasing than anything else until she answered.

Truly, I was undecided myself. Where to fuck Mia tonight? It was the million-dollar question.

"Tell me," I said, dipping my tongue inside her, making her suck in a breath. I closed my fingers around her clit and rubbed while licking her pussy lips before taking the nub into my mouth and sucking hard. Her knees gave way and she reached out to steady herself.

"Easy, girl." Catching her, I rose to stand, bringing her up so that her torso was parallel to the floor. I slid into her pussy while with one hand, I rubbed her clit, and with the other, I played with her nipple, drawing the softest of moans from her.

"Tell me or I'll have to choose," I said, my cock swelling inside her. "I'll give you a hint though. I don't think I'm going to come inside this pussy I'm fucking. Not tonight. And your ass"—I touched two fingers to her back hole and she stiff-ened—"no, it's too sore from the punishment fucking, isn't it?"

She nodded, reaching out to hold onto the back of a chair to steady herself.

"I think," I said, pinching her clit harder, moving a little faster in and out of her. "I think I'll come on your tits and face tonight. We'll see how much I can get into your mouth. Come, Mia, come as you think of how it will feel to be kneeling before me, sucking my cock until I'm ready to explode, then opening your mouth like a good girl while I come all over you."

She gyrated her hips in my hands, fucking my cock as I fucked her, and in the next moment, she came with a deep moan, soaking my cock and fingers, her pussy clamping down around me, making it almost impossible to hold on, to not come inside her then and there.

I pulled out of her and pushed her to her knees at once, stroking my cock quickly as she opened her mouth to take me inside her.

"Good girl." It was more growl than anything else as I gripped the hair at the back of her head and moved her along my length. "That's it, Mia." It wasn't long before I was ready to explode, watching her with her fingers on her pussy as she sucked my cock. "Keep your mouth open, Mia." With that instruction, I pulled out of her, pushing her backward a little, working my cock fast until I came, watching her watch me in fascination as the first spurts of semen splashed across her chest, her neck, her chin and her face before I brought the head of my cock to her mouth. She closed her lips around me while I deposited the rest of my seed onto her hot little tongue, closing my eyes as she milked the last of it from me, leaving me empty.

20

MIA

*J*ulien was distracted. I could hear it in the way he spoke and I could see it on his face.

"Are you worried something will go wrong?" I asked, uncertain. I'd been growing closer and closer to him ever since the day I'd told him everything, so this change, as slight as it was, concerned me.

"What?" He glanced at me quickly before turning his attention back to the road.

Traffic had grown heavier as we neared Rome. Our plan was to pick up the ledger and then head to the airport. We'd booked tickets to Philadelphia already and were scheduled to leave tonight. To say I was nervous was an understatement. Actually, I couldn't even think about that part yet, and I certainly couldn't think of being back in Philadelphia again. I hadn't even called Allison to tell her I was coming. Although I was certain she wasn't involved in that shooting, I intended to keep my promise to Julien.

"You seem worried, that's all."

"No," he patted my knee. "No, I'm not worried. Just thinking things through."

I nodded and looked ahead too. There was more going on, but I had the feeling I should drop it.

"Where will you go when this is over?"

He looked thoughtfully at me, his forehead still creased. "Not sure." He slowed the car as we neared city traffic.

I asked the question without thinking and realized that in a way, I'd grown used to being with him. Would it be strange now to part ways?

"Julien?"

He navigated the car slowly around the busy round-about. "Yes?"

"Will we... I mean, will I have a way to get hold of you? You know, after?"

He seemed to be focused on the driving, but I could see his mind was occupied by more than navigating traffic.

"Why would you want that?" he asked, the change in his tone catching me off guard. He'd reacted sharply, almost snapping at me.

It hurt, but I shrugged my shoulder, not wanting him to see.

Although, maybe he was right. Why would I want that? This was a business arrangement. I would pay him to keep me safe until I claimed my inheritance. That was all. The other stuff, the sex, the *earth-shattering* sex, the punishments even as they intensified everything else — I had to be careful not to misread it. This was only a business arrangement.

"I only meant so that I could wire the money to you and know you got it," I lied.

We came to a standstill at a traffic light and Julien looked over at me, giving me a crooked half smile before pushing the hair out of my face.

"No, you didn't."

He called me out on my lie, making my heart pound against my chest. I didn't know what it was about him but he didn't play games and he didn't waste words. In a way, with Julien, you always knew where you stood. It was just that it sometimes seemed as though where you stood could change at any moment.

"What do you think you want, Mia? Tell me what you think you want out of this."

The light changed then, luckily, and he looked away. Cars honked their horns as Julien unexpectedly changed lanes, and when someone stuck their middle finger up at him, he gave it back, along with what I knew to be choice words in Italian.

"Train station is a few more blocks," he said to me, calm as can be as if nothing had happened.

I nodded, wringing my hands in my lap.

"But I still expect an answer to my question. So, tell me."

"Don't you need to focus on the road?"

"I can do two things at once."

"Sometimes I don't understand you," I said, bluntly. It was true. In some moments, he was so intensely into me that it surprised me how he just switched off.

"What don't you understand?" he asked as he parked the car near the train station.

"Never mind. Nothing." I reached to open the car door but he grasped my other hand to stop me. For a moment, I would have sworn I saw conflict in his eyes, but it was gone quickly.

"Tell me what you don't understand." He held on to me and I knew he would until I answered.

"I know what you are, what you do, but I seem to have come to trust you somehow and I guess..." I paused, searching for the right words, not wanting to make a fool of myself.

"You guess what?"

"I guess I feel hurt when you act cold toward me, that's all."

"You feel hurt?" His eyebrows had gone up as if this were the shock of his life, making me feel even more stupid than I already did.

"Never mind. Let's just go get the ledger." I pushed the door open but he tugged me back and leaned over to my side of the car, his face inches away.

"I like you, Mia. I think you're a sweet girl. Sweet and submissive." With that, his gaze traveled to my lips, then lower to my breasts, which rose and fell with my quick intakes of breath. When he was so close, it was almost too much to take. He had this strange effect on me, always. And yet, he seemed so fully in control, so cool, as if for him, I did nothing at all. As if I meant nothing at all.

Was that where this was going? Was that what I was thinking?

Did I have feelings for him? Is that why I felt hurt at his cool behavior toward me?

His fingers at my chin, caressing my cheek, drew my attention, dragging me back to the present moment. Julien watched me closely, as he always did. He was intense, that was all there was to it. Everything about him was intense and highly charged, almost electric.

"I love the way you blush when I'm close to you." Sliding his hand down over my belly to cup my sex over my jeans, I gasped when he kissed me hard, like every kiss was with him.

I melted against him, closing my eyes and opening my

mouth to him, tasting him, feeling my body surrender to his touch.

With a moan, he slowly broke the kiss and pulled back, his eyes darker, his breath hot. Looking down, he unbuttoned the two buttons at the top of my blouse and pushed it aside to expose one breast.

"Julien, what are you doing? People can see."

I tried to cover myself but he shook his head and took my hand away before sliding the cup of my bra under my breast and licking the nipple. I looked around, out the window, at the street alive with cars and pedestrians.

Julien dipped his head down and licked again, this time closing his mouth over the hardened nipple and drawing it out, the light, soft feel of his tongue circling, sending a charge straight to my clit, making me moan.

He straightened, smiling. "Here comes someone," he said, gesturing with his head in the direction of the man who walked down the street toward where we had parked. He was texting so his attention was absorbed and I straightened to cover myself, but Julien stopped me, taking hold of both of my wrists and watching me.

"No, let him see," he said, unbuttoning one more button and pushing the blouse wider, taking my other breast out from the cup of the bra as well.

"Julien—"

He pinched the newly exposed nipple and it hardened just as the stranger neared our car. The man glanced casually at us, probably caught by the movement in the car. As soon as he saw us though, saw me sitting with my breasts exposed, Julien kissing me softly on my neck, he slowed to look, to watch as Julien licked the length of my collar bone before dipping his head lower and once again taking a nipple into his mouth. His fingers worked slowly to undo my jeans and as he did, I caught the stranger's eye. He seemed shocked at being caught and after a moment, he walked on, fast, just as Julien's fingers slid underneath my panties and closed over my sex.

"You're wet, Mia," he said close to my ear, so close that his breath at my neck made the hairs there stand on end. "Now, tell me what you think you want," he continued, dragging his fingers slowly out of my pants, smearing my juices on my belly before closing my jeans and slowly redressing me.

"I..."

"You think you have feelings for me, is that right?" he asked, a strange smirk on his face, making me wonder about him. He had so many sides to him. So many that frightened me still. "You don't, little Mia." His expression grew completely serious then. "It's the excitement of something new, something dangerous and dirty. Don't confuse sex for anything else. We have a deal. I will keep my end of the bargain, and you will keep yours, and after that, we will say goodbye. There is nothing else to say. You know what I am, and I won't change. Don't fool yourself, Mia."

He was a mercenary. I had to remember that.

"Now," he said, sitting back and taking the keys out of the ignition. "Let's go get that ledger."

21

JULIEN

I got out of the car and shoved my cell phone into my back pocket. I was being a dick but I had to be. She thought she had feelings for me and that shit had to end. Now. I wasn't her lover, and I wasn't her friend. We had a business arrangement and if for one moment I entertained the idea that it was something else, something more, then I was a bigger fool than she.

Cash's email had thrown me for a loop. A million dollars to hand her over to the stepdad. I'd made a deal with Mia but this doubled the money she would or even could pay me. The math was easy.

Fuck.

It should have been easy, and it was pissing me off that it wasn't.

I watched Mia climb out of the car and slam the door shut. Even though I had to squint against the afternoon sun, I knew she wasn't looking at me. She wasn't able to. Well, that was what I'd wanted to achieve, wasn't it? If she hated me, it would be easier, no matter what the fuck I decided to do. We didn't have a future together. I was a hit man. There could be no future with someone like me, not for her. Not for anyone.

I took a step toward her, hating that she shrunk away from me when I did. We walked together without speaking, without really touching even as I guided her toward the station with the barest presence of my fingertips at her back.

"Which locker is it?" I asked once we were inside and walking toward the area where the lockers were.

She searched inside her bag to find her wallet, retrieving the key.

"219." She pointed toward a bank of battered lockers. "There."

I took the key from her, and found the number. The key slid right in and the door opened. There inside was a slimmer than expected leather-bound notebook. I glanced at her to find her eyes wide, staring at the ledger.

"Have you looked inside it?" I asked.

She nodded as I took the book and opened it, just glancing at the handwritten text. Names, numbers and comments, dates, and more dates. Many of the names I recognized.

"Do you know any of the people listed here?"

Mia shook her head. "I don't even want to."

"I think that's smart." I closed the locker and took her by the arm to the café. "Do you want something to eat or drink?"

"I'm not hungry. What are we still doing here? Shouldn't we go?"

"No, we have time — and I need to take care of something first."

Scanning the locker area, I found a little food vendor tucked in a corner. Walking up to the counter, I ordered two sandwiches and two bottles of water.

"I told you I wasn't hungry, Julien," she said when I reached for my wallet to pay.

"You should eat. It'll be a long day and who knows what crap they'll serve on the flight."

"I don't care about that." She looked deflated and it bothered me that I was the cause of that. But I forced that thought aside.

Ignoring her, I gathered the tray and we walked to a table at the very back. There, I set her food out in front of her and took out my phone. First thing I did was send a message to Cash:

How much just for the book?

I then opened the ledger and began to photograph each page, not missing a single one.

"What are you doing?" Mia asked.

"Insurance," I said, snapping another picture before looking up at her. "Eat, Mia."

"Why did you do that?" she asked as she tore back the wrapping on her sandwich.

"Why did I do what?"

Her face flushed red. "Let that man see me."

I took my time, setting the phone down and leaning back in my seat. "I thought it would be the most effective and efficient way to show you your place." I was being an asshole. A fucking asshole with a capital A. "Like I said, Mia, don't confuse things. It won't be good for you to do that."

"I'm not confusing anything, Julien—"

"Oh no?" I leaned in toward her. "Then it must be me."

"Why are you being such a jerk?"

"Because that's what I am, Mia. A jerk. And it would be smart for you to remember that."

"You keep telling me what I should do, what I should think. Well, don't worry. I got the message and I won't forget it. Besides, maybe I'm the one who should remind *you* of *your* place in this. *I* hired *you.* You work for me, asshole!"

Shoving my chair from the table, I got to my feet, picking up the notebook in one hand and dragging Mia up by the other.

"What are you doing?" She tried to push my hand off of her, but she wasn't strong enough. Not nearly.

Other patrons looked at us but I ignored them as we walked toward the restrooms, taking the key from the counter as we passed it and going into the men's room.

"Get your jeans down and bend over," I told her after locking the door.

"No! You're fucking insane or bipolar or something with all your fucking mood swings!"

"I have to admit," I said, gripping her arm again and undoing her jeans with the other hand. "I like it when you fight me."

She struggled, making it hard to yank the tight jeans off. "Stop! You're crazy. People will hear."

"You should have thought of that before."

I switched on the fan to muffle any sound and turned her, forcing her to bend over the sink and yanking her jeans down over her hips.

"I hate you."

I wanted to say that it didn't matter. That all that mattered was the fact that I was the one keeping her alive. But I didn't because it didn't fucking matter.

I pushed her panties down and undid my jeans, one hand pressing between her shoulder blades even before she'd stopped struggling. I wasn't even hard, hating what I was about to do, hating myself for it. But I had not fucking choice.

She needed to see who I was. What I was. It would make things easier later.

I rubbed my cock against her pussy, and slowly pushed inside her, forcing myself to look at her only to find her watching me in the mirror.

Those eyes, those fucking eyes, even now, even given what I was doing to her, inside them wasn't the hate that I expected. That I fucking deserved.

I gripped a handful of hair, tugging her head backwards, hurting her. I forced myself to watch her as I fucked her made myself look at the hurt in her eyes, wanting to make her hate me. Needing to make her hate me.

Just a few thrusts. It was al it took. She squeezed her eyes shut when I fisted the handful of hair as I neared my climax closing my own eyes. Coming.

This was fucked up. I was fucked up.

I loosened my grip and opened my eyes, meeting my own reflection in the mirror. If I'd had any hope of redemption before, it was gone now. Gone as Mia's body went limp. She could never forgive me this. I knew it.

And I hated myself for it.

"Julien."

My vision blurred and I quickly swiped the back of my hadn't over my eyes before looking at her. I pulled out, tucked myself back into my jeans, all the while memorizing those eyes, the look inside them.

Because what I saw wasn't what I expected. What I deserved.

I pulled her upright and turned her to face me, unable to look away, because there, reflected back, was me. Not as I was. Not as I saw myself. But as she saw me.

She held onto hope. She still clung to it like a fucking life raft in the middle of the ocean. But the truth was, there was no hope. Not for me. I wasn't good and I certainly wasn't good enough —not for her. I'd known it all along but seeing her now, after the way I'd been treating her, after what I'd just done to her, she was ready to forgive me. She desperately wanted for me to be good.

But I wasn't.

I wrapped my hand around the back of her little neck. Christ, she was so fragile, I could snap it in a second. Anyone could.

I brought my forehead to hers, pressing her back against the wall. I couldn't stop looking at those eyes, at the hope there, the promise of something I didn't deserve, not in this lifetime. Probably not in the next either, if there really was such a thing as Karma.

I held her like that for a long time. Her hands came up along my back, and she pulled me closer, smearing tears across her cheek and mine. I wasn't sure whose they were anymore.

"I'm sorry." My voice cracked as I made my pathetic apology, but she only pulled me closer and held me.

A knock interrupted us, but I ignored it, holding her tighter. But when it came again, I cleared my throat and straightened, releasing her and reaching for the door.

"Get yourself together. We leave in two minutes."

22

MIA

I didn't know what it was, what was going on in his head. Even when he seemed to be angry with me, even when he said he was showing me my place, I knew he was angry with himself, was trying to keep me at arm's length because maybe, just maybe, he couldn't trust himself. Julien had feelings for me — he had to. What we'd shared, it couldn't be one-sided. And all I could think was that he was acting in the only way he knew how: he was pushing me away because he couldn't handle those feelings.

I'd thought he would kiss me. If he'd kissed me, it would have made all the difference. He wouldn't be able to hide then. I wouldn't let him. I'd be strong enough for the both of us, if that's what it took.

In the time we'd been together, I felt like I knew more about him than anyone else in the world. He had trusted me enough to tell me about his brother. I saw the pain, the guilt he felt over Charlie's death, and, perhaps subconsciously, he'd wanted me to see it. He'd wanted, or maybe even needed, to share that pain. In a way, we'd found a kindred spirit in each other, he in me, and me in him. Our guilt and our pain connected us.

Someone knocked on the door.

"Just a minute."

I pulled my panties and jeans up, and splashed water on my face. I could forgive him so much, if only he'd let me. I finally admitted it to myself as I hurriedly cleaned up, the gravity, the meaning of it stunning me.

I loved Julien.

It made no sense — none of this did — but I had fallen in love with him when that had been the farthest thing from my mind. I knew when it was too, down to the very moment I knew I loved him. It was when he'd made that dinner for us after I'd told him about Jason. After he'd held me and I'd wept like I hadn't wept in too long, not even at my sister's memorial. Things had shifted between us that night. And I couldn't be the only one who felt that. I just couldn't.

Taking a deep breath, I pulled the door open. The man who'd knocked raised his eyebrows and I remembered Julien had taken us to the men's room. I didn't care though, and as I walked, I determined not to look at anyone. Even as I felt eyes on me, I only concentrated on Julien's deep blue ones, those dark, shadowed eyes that held mine as I made my way to our table.

"I wrapped up your sandwich," Julien said.

"Thanks." I shoved it into my purse though I had no intention of eating it.

"Ready?" he asked, his tone tender and quiet. Something had changed.

I nodded and he rose. This time, he didn't take my arm like he had earlier. Instead, he folded his big hand around mine, and even though he struggled to meet my gaze, there was something in the wya he held me. Perhaps words he wasn't able to say, perhaps just guilt. It didn't matter. All that mattered was the way he held on to me now.

Like this, we walked to the car and drove in silence to the airport.

§&

THE FLIGHT TO PHILADELPHIA WAS FULL. JULIEN HAD BOOKED first-class seats, which was good as it gave us privacy, even though something told me we wouldn't be talking much. In fact, Julien closed his eyes as soon as we sat down. He wasn't asleep, I could tell that, but I could also tell he didn't want to talk.

I was anxious. I was due to pick up the money soon, which meant whatever was going to happen was going to happen then. The more I thought of it, the more I knew neither Jason nor his dad would miss the opportunity to see me. If it were up to me, that would be their last chance because if this succeeded, if I got that money, I was disappearing for good. I trusted that Julien could keep me safe. If anyone could, it would be him. But I didn't want to underestimate the St. Roses — and that ledger was worrisome. I wondered if Tanya hadn't stolen it if they would have let me be, forgotten me by now. That million couldn't matter to them, not with the amounts I knew they had.

Julien stirred beside me. "I'm going to run to the restroom. Stay here."

"Okay." Where would I go? I shrugged a shoulder and turned the page on the magazine that sat open on my lap, the one I'd picked up but hadn't really looked at. It hadn't been a moment since he'd been gone that a sound from his seat caught my attention and I saw that he'd left his phone there. It had probably slid out of his back pocket when he sat down.

I picked it up, intending to give it to him when he returned and wanting to make sure he didn't sit on it. I hadn't planned on reading the message on the screen:

"It's a package deal. He wants the girl AND the book."

What?

I looked up to make sure he was still in the bathroom and opened the email to read the previous messages. What I saw chilled me to the bone.

Julien had a new job and that job... was me. He'd been hired to deliver me along with the ledger to Samuel St. Rose.

I heard Julien's voice then and saw he was talking to one of the flight attendants. Quickly glancing at the date of the mail, I set the phone back on his seat and focused my attention on the magazine on my lap. I tried to smile when he sat back down, but it was almost impossible. Even looking at him hurt me.

All I could see was betrayal, finally understanding why he'd been acting like he had.

And he was right. I was a fool.

Julien scrolled through some screens and I assumed he was going through his e-mail. He read without any expression on his face and the only thing I saw when he looked back at me was the smallest suggestion of regret, but even that was quickly wiped away.

I knew that he was my enemy now. He was going to deliver me to Samuel and Jason. Even if he had been planning on helping me at first, Samuel had doubled the money I had offered, taking me out of the game altogether.

I closed the magazine and turned to look out the window as the attendants closed the aircraft door. Resting my head against the seat, I closed my eyes, trying to process, trying to figure out what I was going to do next. I was on my own. Completely. And there was only one person I could reach out to, even if Julien didn't trust her, even if he'd tried to cast doubt on her.

It was Allison.

Now that I knew whose side Julien was really on, it vindicated Allison in my eyes. For a moment, my mind tried to do the same for him, erase the guilt that belonged to him, but I wouldn't allow it. Not even when I thought about how he'd changed toward me. How he'd been so caring, even loving — before that email.

I shook my head, banishing those thoughts.

I was finished being a gullible fool.

He was an assassin, a hired gun. And I'd now become his next target.

I had just eight hours to plan my escape from him because I knew now I was no longer his to protect. I was his prisoner, and he was a mercenary. He'd chosen the highest bidder, even knowing what Jason had done to me. At least I knew where I stood now. That had to mean something, even if my chest hurt a little at the betrayal I felt.

ONCE WE LANDED, WE MOVED QUICKLY THROUGH THE immigration line using the automated passport check. I didn't know Julien's last name. He'd never told it to me, and a peek at his passport didn't answer any questions because there by a photo of him wearing a pair of dark rimmed glasses was the name David Sullivan.

He caught my puzzled look and smiled. "Ready, honey?"

"Yep." I smiled right back. Everything about this man was a lie. *He* was a lie.

Once we were cleared via the machines, an agent collected the printout and gave us both a once over before sending us through without a problem.

I wondered if Julien was nervous at all. On the outside, he smiled and looked relaxed. He even slipped on the glasses from the photo which made him look a little older, but no less handsome. I didn't want to find him handsome though. I wanted to hate him. To remember what he was, what he was going to do.

He kept the ledger in a black leather backpack he carried and I eyed it while we waited for the one bag we'd checked. It was nearly empty but it would have looked suspicious if we'd come without checked luggage, so we'd brought it along.

"What now?" I asked.

"We'll go to the hotel for the night. See the city. Have a nice dinner."

My last supper.

"And then?"

He flashed that dark little grin, the one that made my belly flutter, made my heart race at the anticipation of things to come.

As if sensing what he was doing to me, he stepped close, a hand coming to cup the back of my head. "And then we fuck." His breath at my ear made me shudder. "Or we can skip all of it and get right to the fucking."

At my look, Julien laughed and pulled me close. "There's our bag."

I didn't understand this, didn't understand him. He was the perfect Judas. He would betray me easily, even with a kiss, as though what had happened in that bathroom in Rome hadn't happened at all.

I watched him as he moved through the crowd gathered

at the luggage carousel. People got out of Julien's way, always. He easily picked up the bag, keeping the backpack on his shoulder all along. He brushed the hair back from his face and gestured to me.

"Come, Mia."

I went obediently, his hand at my back as we easily passed through customs, handing in one more form to a final agent before making our way out to the waiting taxis. The late afternoon sky was muggy as usual in this city, and the old smells and sounds were something I hadn't missed. In fact, being there only made me want to leave.

Philadelphia held bad memories for me.

Climbing into a cab, Julien told the driver the name of the hotel and turned to me. "Your sister's memorial is here, isn't it?"

The question caught me off guard, but I nodded.

"Do you want to go see it?"

This might be my one opportunity to make an escape, even though I wasn't sure I did want to go. It wasn't like she was there. "Maybe, but on my own."

I needed to get that ledger. I had a plan. If all went well at the attorney, I would leave it for Samuel. If not, well, I'd hand it over myself, a show of good faith, and ask him to leave me alone. To keep his son away from me. The thought that it might be Jason waiting for me there was one I couldn't entertain.

But it turned out it didn't matter anyway because Julien shook his head.

"No way. We'll be stuck like glue until those papers are signed."

"Why? No one knows I'm back, right?"

What was I doing? I did not need him to suspect that I knew, that I'd read his email.

"I'm not willing to take any chances. They found you in Italy. Twice."

"Are you sure that second time was about me? I mean, haven't you made some enemies?" I left out the 'in your line of work', remembering what that had gotten me the last time.

"Not possible. I'm invisible."

"That's right, David Sullivan."

"Something wrong?" he asked. "You seem on edge."

I looked out the window as we drove into the city. It was just as I remembered it: noisy, dirty and busy, full of cars and people.

"Just anxious."

"We'll take care of that anxiety in a minute." His hand settled on my leg, moving up along my inner thigh.

I looked at it, then caught the eye of the driver on us in the rear view mirror. I put my hand on top of Julien's. "Stop." I tried to pull his hand off, but he gripped my thigh when I did, hurting me.

"I'll stop when I'm ready to stop."

It was like a showdown. I glared, wanting to scream at him, to shake him, ask him what he was thinking. But I didn't, and he won in the end. When I dropped my gaze, he released my leg.

"We're here," Julien said.

The driver turned off at the Marriott. Julien climbed out, grabbing the backpack as he did, and paid the driver. I waited while they unloaded our bag and then followed Julien inside, yawning. I was tired. I'd not slept more than an hour or two on the flight, and wanted a shower and a comfortable bed.

I watched Julien as he checked us in, realizing I'd be sharing the bed with him.

The front desk agent handed over a package, and, taking our keys, Julien gestured for me to go ahead. We took the elevator up to our room on the seventeenth floor, a large but unremarkable room with one king size bed.

Julien set down the suitcase and the backpack.

"What's in the box?" I asked.

He smiled at me and opened it, taking out a black revolver similar to the one he'd had in Italy.

"Can't travel with these, so I had one delivered."

Checking on what I assumed was the ammunition, he set the pistol down casually and went over to the window to take in the view. I joined him. This was how I liked the city: dusk bathing it in its eerie glow. It was the only way I liked it. Without sound, people and cars and trucks all moved like ants below us. Julien took hold of my hand, intertwining his fingers with mine. I looked at it, this tender gesture, but he kept his gaze out the window.

I didn't understand this man. Was it regret? Was it the knowledge that soon, he would deliver me to those who would harm me? Would he leave me at their mercy? Could he?

I slid my hand out of his. "I'm going to have a shower."

He turned to me. If he knew something was up, he didn't give it away. But he was a man used to reading people, to watching them for the slightest changes in behavior.

"All right."

I wasn't sure what I expected, why *I* felt guilty, duplicitous.

Before I let on what was on my mind, I walked to the bathroom where I took my time in the shower, working on autopilot, washing my hair, conditioning, not sure how things were going to go once I got out there. But it turned out I didn't have to wait to find out because the shower door slid open, startling me. I was about to protest when Julien's big, naked body took up most of the space inside the shower. Before I could utter a sound, he was on me, pushing me against the tiles, his mouth crashing onto mine in a deep kiss that stole my breath in its ferocity. He cupped the back of my head, and where I was used to his fingers tangling in my hair and pulling, this time, he held me, cushioning my head against the hard tiles.

I could do nothing but open to him, my body used to his, to him. His hard, naked chest pressed against mine and water from the shower splashed along our shoulders, his back. His kiss was long and slow, penetrating but not taking, softening and deepening at once, not quite devouring but having me all the same. It aroused, but he always aroused me. Being around him, my body worked from memory and I found my hands, which had at first pushed against his chest, now softened, exploring the hard muscle instead, curling over big shoulders and biceps.

He ground against me, that kiss deepening, his cock pressing against my belly, hard against soft, and one hand moved to my hip as he released my mouth and turned his attention to my neck, to that hollow at my collarbone, and he bit, sending my belly fluttering, making me wrap my hands over his shoulders and grip. It didn't hurt, the bite, it only aroused as he kissed, then bit again at the curve of my neck and back, drawing me closer to him, that hand at my hip now lifting my leg until I wrapped it and the other around his hips. His cock stood at the entrance of my pussy when he returned his mouth to mine, his eyes open this time.

"I want you, Mia. I want to make love to you."

Make love.

He'd never said those words before and I'd never call

what we did making love. We fucked. We fucked like wild beasts fucked and he got off on it. I got off on it. But now, looking into the deep blue depths of his eyes, I saw tenderness along with that fiery passion — and all I could do was kiss him, open to him, tell him without a single word *yes*.

He slid the shower door open, and, leaving the water running, he carried me toward the bed, kissing me as we dripped all over the carpet, depositing me onto the bed soaking wet and laying his weight on top of me.

"I want it," I said when he lifted himself up onto elbows, nudging my legs apart with his knees. "I want your weight. I want to feel all of you."

"You won't be able to breathe," he said, kissing me, giving me more of his weight but not all of it. Not yet.

"All of it. I want all of it, Julien. I don't want to breathe."

Was it true? Was that what I wanted?

He looked at me, his eyes shining. He heard my words and watched my eyes as I watched him. His cock slid slowly inside me, stretching me, making me gasp like it always did when he first entered me. Once I'd drawn that breath, he gave me what I wanted. Lifting me higher onto the bed, he lay his weight on me and began to fuck me slowly, shifting his hips a little, hitting just the right spot.

"Kiss me, Julien."

He'd been watching me until then, our faces inches apart, our gazes locked. He gave me what I asked for, but neither of us closed our eyes when he brought his mouth to mine and I felt the shift as he lifted up a little, giving my lungs room to take in breath while he pushed deeper inside me, our bodies touching at every possible point.

When his movements came just a little faster, he pulled back and watched my face again. We stayed like that, making slow love, not once taking our eyes off one another, almost like we both knew it would be the last time. And when he swelled inside me, he reached to take one leg higher, penetrating deeper, the thrusts coming shorter, harder now.

Pressure built and built as he watched me. I came just moments before him and when I let out a long sigh, it seemed to signal his own release. His eyes glittered, black centers ringed with the brightest blue, his face different, unearthly almost, as he thrust once more then stilled inside me, filling me, making me feel whole and complete.

It was long moments afterwards when my body cooled, sweat chilly against my skin, reality weighing upon my heart once more.

There was nothing right about this — or if there had been, it wasn't anymore. If it ever had a chance, he'd ruined it. And for what?

For money.

"I'm cold," I said, squirming out from under him.

He rolled off, surprised.

I walked toward the bathroom where the water still ran, all while his seed slid down my inner thighs, and I climbed back into the shower, scrubbing his scent from me, wanting to wash his slow love making from my memory. It tasted of deception, and his betrayal turned my stomach.

As my tears mixed with the quickly cooling water, I knew I wouldn't be able to wash away the memory of him, of his eyes, his touch, his smell. None of it. I was fucked. I loved a killer, a man who would deliver me to my death if I didn't find some way to get away from him, try to fix the mess I was in, and finally, permanently, disappear.

23

JULIEN

*W*hile Mia washed, I picked up my cell phone and reread that message a hundred times, thinking about my options.

If asked even a few weeks ago, I would have laughed at the ludicrous notion that I'd even be considering a girl over a million dollars. But today, I wasn't laughing. I looked up at the closed door of the bathroom and thought of her.

Fuck!

If I handed her over, it wouldn't matter if Samuel didn't hurt her — because Jason would. If I helped her to get to the attorney to sign the paperwork, they'd be waiting. I wasn't foolish enough to think otherwise, and neither was Mia. If we just disappeared, we'd be on the run for the rest of our lives.

I picked up the hotel room phone and dialed my grandmother. It was early, but she answered, annoyed at being woken, which was kind of funny, considering. She was a tough lady, and if anyone went out there to do any damage, they'd have to reckon not only with her, but the entire village. The image of it made me smile, but then the shower switched off and I thought of the bigger problem at hand.

Getting up, I opened the suitcase and picked out fresh clothes for Mia and myself, waiting for her to emerge from the bathroom.

"Any hot water left?" I asked in the hopes of breaking through the heavy mood that had settled around us.

"Probably not." She looked at the dress I held out for her. "No, I don't want to get dressed and go out. I'm just going to try to get some sleep."

"It's too early for that, and you need to eat. Besides, I need to ask you some questions about Samuel. Let me have a shower and we'll grab a quick bite and talk."

"Julien, please. I don't want to."

"You don't have a choice, Mia. Now, are you going to be here when I get out or do I need to bind you to the bed like the first time we were in a hotel room?"

I didn't miss her quick glance at the backpack. "I'll be here. Go ahead."

I went to her and took her arms, rubbing the goose bumps away. "You okay?"

"I'm anxious. I want this to be done."

"Try to relax."

"Easier said than done."

"I'm not going to let anything happen to you, Mia."

Her brow furrowed at that and her gaze darted away.

"Do you trust me?" I asked, squeezing her arms until she looked at me.

Her eyes searched mine and I could see her struggle. "Can I?"

Could she?

"I guess only you can decide that."

Non answer.

Releasing her, I glanced at the backpack but purposely left it where it was and headed into the bathroom. I kept the door open and watched as best as I could while having the quickest shower ever, barely giving her time to get dressed. The fact that the backpack was where she could have grabbed it and ran, spoke to the fact that she should trust me. Not that I'd truly let her go anywhere with that book. It wasn't the right thing to do. Hell, her options were so limited, but on her own, she was dead. With me, she might have a chance.

Now, I just had to decide what the fuck I was doing — how I was going to keep her alive *and* get that million.

24

MIA

*D*id I trust him?

I looked at the backpack as I dressed, hurrying, glancing at the shower as I pulled the dress he'd chosen for me over my head, weighing my options. If I ran now, it might give me a few minutes head start, but I wouldn't put it past him to chase me down the hall naked. Then he'd be pissed.

But it turned out I didn't have to decide on anything much because he finished showering in record time and I saw how intensely he looked at me when he stepped out, even as he made some small joke to try to lighten the mood.

He knew I didn't trust him and he obviously didn't trust me.

I dried my hair, and pulled it into a ponytail. Then we headed out for dinner, Julien carrying the backpack with him. He wasn't taking any chances, and I wondered if he'd sleep with that ledger under his pillow.

He chose a Chinese place nearby. It was quiet and dark, which was perfect. We ordered our meals and Julien took my hands.

"Tell me about Samuel. Tell me about how he was with your sister, with you."

"Why?"

"I want to know who I'll potentially be dealing with."

"You say *potentially*, but you don't mean it, do you? I mean, it's unlikely that they'll *not* show up. They'll know when I reach the attorney's office. I can't imagine he wouldn't tip them off."

"I think it's wise for us to assume that. That's why I want to know about Samuel."

"Not Jason?"

"No. He's the less interesting of the two. Jason's type I know. Hot headed, not very smart, predictable. Birthright is the only reason he's where he is. He's Samuel St. Rose's only son."

"I never got the feeling there was much love between Samuel and Jason. Until push came to shove, I guess."

"How was Samuel with Tanya? Did he love her?"

It was strange hearing her name spoken aloud. "I thought so. She was younger than him by a lot, only a year older than Jason. She could have been his daughter. Tanya and I were alone from the time I was eight. She was thirteen. We came from a bad home — usual story. Drunk for a mom and dad MIA from as far back as I can remember. We ran away and somehow managed to stay gone, stay out of the system. We lived on the streets, but we survived. Samuel managed to earn her trust somehow and she looked at him like he was a king, a god. She wanted to please him.

"I'd had her to rely on. She'd had no one, not until Samuel came along, and that meant something to both of them. Who knows, maybe Samuel just liked having this young, beautiful girl looking at him the way Tanya did. I don't know what it was, but I did think his love for her was genuine."

"How did she meet Samuel?"

I looked at him before answering, then dropped my gaze.

"I won't judge. I know what it feels like to be hungry, Mia. I know what I've done out of desperation."

God, it sounded like he already knew. "She was an escort. High end." I shrugged my shoulder, hating that she'd had to do that and that she'd been doing it from too early an age. "Samuel was a client."

Julien nodded. "Go on."

"He was her last client. He treated her well, really well. Bought her anything she even looked at twice, took her out all the time, liked showing her off. She was pretty — really pretty." My sister had been happy then, the happiest I'd ever seen her. We hadn't had anything growing up and Samuel, well, he turned that around, showing us a lifestyle neither of us had ever even imagined.

"And how was he with you?"

"He was nice to me. Nicer to me than I was to him. On the one hand, I was happy to see my sister so happy, but on the other... I felt like he was taking her away from me, in a way."

"Taking her love?"

"She said no, that it wasn't true. And I guess it wasn't. She was young though. I always forgot that. She was more like a mom than a sister to me. I think it was that someone was taking care of her for the first time and not wanting anything back in exchange, you know?" I shrugged as the waitress set our food down. I picked up my chopsticks and watched Julien take his fork. "I think people — men — always wanted something from her."

"Not all men are like that."

"Aren't they?"

He ignored that. "Do you think he would hurt you, Mia? Samuel, I mean."

I set my chopsticks down and sat back, folding my hands in my lap. "There was a time he would have done anything for my sister, but I wasn't there for a long time, not at the end. They'd sent me away. I want to believe that he wouldn't, but I don't want to be stupid. Besides, he chose Jason over me once, even knowing what he'd done to me."

"But do you think he could or would hurt you? Say if you gave the ledger back and promised to disappear?"

"I don't know."

"That doesn't help."

"Why are you asking, anyway?"

"Because he hired me to find you, Mia. He's offered to pay me one million dollars to deliver you and the ledger to him."

I sat shocked for a long moment. Even though I already knew this, to hear him say it aloud was something else — and I never for one second expected him to say it.

He'd come clean. That meant something, didn't it?

Don't be a fucking fool!

"I know."

He sat back then. "That's why you've been acting like you have."

"What do you plan to do?"

"Well, ideally, I'd love to get the money *and* help you disappear — but that may not be as easy as I'd like."

"No shit."

"Believe it or not, Mia, I don't want to see you get hurt."

"But you'd look the other way for a million bucks?"

He studied me through narrowed eyes, and shoved a

forkful of food into his mouth. "Why do you think I'm telling you? If I was going to do it, don't you think I'd keep my mouth shut about the job?"

I pushed soggy rice soaked in too much sauce around my plate. "You know what?" I set my chopsticks down and put my napkin on the table. "I don't know, Julien. I don't have a fucking clue. I can't figure you out. One minute, you're nice to me. The next, you're a total dick."

Calm and cool as I'd ever seen him, he shoved another forkful into his mouth and nodded, as if agreeing. I just didn't get the guy.

"I'd be lying if I said the thought of handing you over for a million bucks didn't tempt me."

That *did* scare me — and the fact that he could so casually say it terrified me.

"Don't look like that, Mia," he said, taking a bite of an eggroll. "I didn't say I was going to do it."

"Okay, then tell me. Just tell me where I stand, because right now, I don't know. Don't fucking toy with me on this, Julien. It's not fair." I swiped the back of my hand across my eyes, hating that I cried when I was upset, worked up, anxious — anything at all!

"Christ, isn't it obvious yet? Are you that thick?" he said this with a tap on the side of my head.

"I guess I am. Just spell it out."

"No, Mia. I'm not going to hand you over to a step-brother who raped and beat you, nor to a stepdad who may have reason to hurt you."

"Why not? I can't pay you a million dollars! I probably won't be able to pay you the half I promised!"

"Jesus!" He reached over the small table and grabbed the back of my head, pulling me to him. "Somehow, someway, you've managed to work your way under my skin, Mia St.

Rose, and I'd kill them before I'd let them touch a hair on your head. Is that clear enough?"

My mouth dropped open, and he shook his head.

"I care about you," he said.

I stared at him, my mind reeling.

"How it's come to that, I haven't a fucking clue. But there it is." He shoved a final forkful of food into his mouth, wiped his lips and sat back, tossing the napkin onto his plate and glaring at me. "Not a single clue."

Well, that was certainly not what I'd expected to hear.

"You finished here?" It was the waitress. Julien smiled politely, but I could see he was annoyed.

"I'll take the check," he said, taking out his wallet. His eyes were on me the entire time. "Nothing to say?" he asked once she'd left with our plates.

I shook my head with a loud exhale. "I'm... surprised, I guess. No. Shocked."

The waitress dropped the check on the table on her way by. Julien looked it over and slipped a few bills into the folder before rising. "Shocked, huh? Well, me too."

I slipped my hand into his and we walked quietly out of the restaurant and back to the hotel. We planned on being at the attorney's office by 10:00 AM and it was almost 11:00 PM. Less than twelve hours to go.

"Relax, Mia," Julien urged once we were in the elevator. "You're practically shaking."

I smiled, but it was forced. "I want this over." Hadn't I said that before?

The elevator stopped and the doors slid quietly open. Julien led the way to our room and once we were inside, he locked it and set the backpack down.

"Strip off your clothes." He said it casually while he took his jacket off.

"I'm not really in the mood..."

He took two steps toward me, his eyes locked on mine. "Strip."

As if to help me, he reached back to unzip the dress. "I'm trying to decide," he said, as the dress slid off my shoulders and pooled around my ankles. He turned me around and unhooked my bra, then pushed the straps down over my arms before cupping my breasts in his hands, pulling me to him so his cock pressed against my back. "Pussy," he continued, his hands sliding to my panties, pushing them down to just beneath my hips, one hand cupping my sex. "Or ass." His other cupped my bottom before slipping between my cheeks to smear the juices up to that tight ring, circling there, making my breath come fast.

"But first," he said, turning me around to kiss me, walking me backward until the backs of my knees hit the bed. "Get on the bed and open your legs wide. I want to have a taste of your pussy." He pushed me down so I sat on the edge of the bed. I stared up at him as he tugged his t-shirt off, the sight of his naked chest always doing a number on me, making me want like I'd never wanted anyone else before.

My gaze slid down to his pants as he undid them and slid them and his underwear to the floor before peeling my panties —which were still around my thighs — off. With a finger at my chest, he pushed me back to lie down, raising my legs as he knelt between them, looking at my exposed, open cunt.

"You look so good, and you smell even better," he said before taking one long lick. "But the way you taste, Mia. It's something else entirely."

With a moan, I reached my hands to his head, fingers twining through thick hair, pulling him to me.

"That feels... so... good." He licked and sucked, his mouth soft, the stubble on his face rough in contrast, and when he rubbed his chin against my clit, God, I almost died. One finger slid into my pussy and the other circled my ass. When he penetrated there, he closed his mouth over my clit and sucked hard, pushing me over the edge. The muscles of my pussy and ass clenched around his fingers as I pulled him tight to me, my eyes closed, pressing his face into me until my entire being became throbbing sensation.

He pulled away when I loosened my hold on him, my legs going limp around him. Julien rose to his feet as I watched him. His lips curved in a smile that I returned, he then rolled me over onto my belly, shoving pillows beneath my hips, raising them high. I lay my face down on the cool sheets, watching as he went into the bathroom and returned with the small bottle of lotion. He stood, rubbing a generous amount over the length of his cock, his eyes drinking in my exposed ass before meeting my gaze.

"I've decided," he said, adjusting my position a little, widening the spread of my legs as he stood between them.

I knew what he wanted and hollowed out my back to offer it to him.

"I love your ass, Mia," he said, emptying the bottle of moisturizer at the base of my spine before smearing it down toward my asshole, the lotion cold as he covered me with it. "Spread your cheeks open for me. Offer me your ass to fuck."

I was dripping again and I didn't hesitate to obey. Reaching back, I spread myself open and watched him look at me, his gaze going dark, his cock thickening even more.

"That's it," he said. "Just a little wider so I can see that tight little hole."

He rubbed more lotion over his cock with one hand,

while with the other, he began to push the stuff inside me, his fingers sliding in easily with all of the slippery cream, the sensations driving me insane.

"Fuck me, please, Julien." I pulled my bottom cheeks wider, wanting him, arching my back even more. I watched him as he brought his cock to my ass, lining the thick head up against the tight hole. I tensed for a moment, knowing there would be pain at first, but remembering the orgasms that came with this kind of fucking. I pushed against him when he pressed against my hole, stretching me open. I closed my eyes, and we stilled, me on the verge of another orgasm as my clit pressed against the pillows and my body softened against the intrusion of his too big, too thick cock.

Before I was ready, he pushed some more, making me grunt.

"Get up on your forearms and face forward now, Mia. Brace yourself because I need to fuck this tight little hole hard." He spoke while pushing in deeper, stretching me wider while I pulled my forearms underneath me, looking straight ahead as ordered, trying to keep my bottom relaxed — and trying even harder not to come for as long as possible. I knew that once I did, I'd be ultra sensitive.

"That's it, just relax your ass. I'm about half way, Mia, and I can't wait to feel your hot little walls stretched tight around my cock. I can't wait to come inside your ass."

That did it, because when he pushed in farther, I moved my hips just a little, arching my back some more, the action causing my clit to rub against the pillows, bringing on the first of several orgasms. I cried out and he pushed in all the way in one hard thrust as I came, filling me fully. He remained still while I came that first time, my walls squeezing tight around him. When I looked over my shoulder and saw his eyes on my ass, a fleeting feeling of jealousy bloomed within me, wanting to watch too. I wanted to see his cock disappear into my ass. I wanted to watch it thrust in and out of me, and I wanted to take his cum and keep it inside me — keep some part of him with me forever.

He met my gaze and gave me that one-sided grin before gripping my hips. He pulled my cheeks wide and drew out, holding there for a moment before thrusting in hard. I gripped the sheets, making all kinds of noises while I rubbed my clit against the pillows, pushing back against him, meeting his thrusts, the lotion, combined with his pre-cum, leaving my passage slippery, easing his way. I came again with a groan, and this time, he continued to fuck me as I did. Then, with a cry more like an animal's growl, he thrust brutally before stilling inside me, his cock throbbing as I came one final time, feeling him empty inside me.

He pulled out of me slowly, and I felt every inch of his slippery retreat.

"Stay," he said, one hand at my back, his eyes on my ass. "I want to watch."

I knew what he liked. Even as it embarrassed me, this act of submission aroused me too, and I did as he said, keeping my bottom presented to him as his seed slipped from inside me, my face reddening as, still warm and slippery, it dripped down my inner thigh, until there was no more.

Finally raising me from the bed, he carried me to the bathroom and washed me in the bath before washing himself off. I was spent, empty, and I nearly fell asleep with my head on his shoulder as he carried me back to the bed.

He climbed in beside me, holding my back to his front as I floated off to sleep.

It was a little after 5:00 AM when I woke. Julien was sound asleep beside me. Across the room, the backpack lay on its side on top of the dresser.

I turned slowly so as not to wake him, but remained there looking at Julien, watching him breathe, his mouth slightly open. I remembered the time we'd been in that first hotel room, how he'd had that nightmare — and I realized it hadn't occurred since. I thought about what he'd said last night. He cared about me. I wondered if maybe that was his way of saying he loved me.

I shook off that thought, and quietly climbed out of the bed.

Thing was, I cared for him too. I trusted him and believed what he had told me last night was the truth. And that was why it was even more important I did what I was about to do. Samuel or Jason — or both — would be waiting for me today. I couldn't stand it if something happened to Julien because of me — and something *would* happen. I had to take care of this myself. It was time to stop running, stop hiding, and put all of this behind me.

The clothes I'd worn on our flight still hung over the back of a chair and I quickly dressed. I thought about leaving a note, but that would take too much time and I couldn't take a chance that Julien would wake, so I picked up my shoes and the backpack, glanced once more at the still sleeping Julien, and as quietly as I could, left the room.

The elevator was too close and I was afraid he'd hear the dinging sound when it arrived, so instead of that, I opted to take the stairs all the way down, tripping twice in my rush. Now that I'd left, adrenaline pumped through my system, filling me with energy. At the ground floor, I unzipped the little pocket of the backpack where I found Julien's wallet and our passports. I hated to do it, but, taking most of the cash out, I asked for an envelope at the front desk where I left his passport and wallet for him along with instructions to leave him a message that the package was here.

I walked outside, declining the bellhop's offer to call a taxi, and grabbed a cab farther down the street myself, giving the driver the address to the cemetery. I didn't want to take a chance that the bellhop would be able to tell Julien where I was going.

I looked behind me once on our way out, but aside from that, I forced myself to focus on what lay ahead, both hands holding onto the backpack that sat on my lap, the ledger feeling far heavier than it actually was.

I'd left my own wallet and cell phone behind, but I didn't need either. I had my passport and within a few hours, I'd either be a free woman with a substantial amount of money to her name — or a dead one. I wondered if dead was an exaggeration, but didn't dwell on it.

When we got to the cemetery half an hour later, I asked the driver to wait for me. I couldn't stay long, but needed to come in case I didn't get a chance for a longer visit later.

25

JULIEN

*W*hen I got my hands on Mia, I was going to kill her.

The blinking of the message light woke me a little after 6:00 AM. How I slept through her leaving, I had no idea. Well, it went to show how much I trusted the girl. Shaking my head, I tied my shoelaces, loaded and tucked my new revolver into the back of my jeans and went downstairs.

"I'm David Sullivan. I had a message someone had left a package for me?"

"Yes, Mr. Sullivan. Just a moment." The agent went to the back office and quickly returned with a large envelope. I turned away and tore it open, finding my passport and wallet inside. Nothing else, no note, no thank you, no sorry, no... nothing.

"Were you here when this was left?"

"Yes, sir. She asked that we not disturb you for an hour. I hope it wasn't too early."

"Where did she go?"

"Oh, I don't know, sir. Perhaps the bellhop might

remember." He raised a hand, calling toward the front doors. "Vincent?"

The bellhop came over. "A young woman from about an hour ago? Dark hair, attractive? Do you remember her?"

"Oh. Yes, sir. I remember."

"Where was she going?" I asked, irritated by the slow response.

"That I don't know. She didn't say much to me, I'm afraid."

Crap.

"Did she take a taxi? Perhaps you can call and find out where they were headed?" I suggested.

He shook his head. "No, sir. She walked off and I saw her climb into a taxi down the street."

"Which way? Do you remember the direction the taxi took?"

She'd purposely not taken a taxi from the hotel.

"Yes, sir." He pointed. That was all I got — an idiot pointing the way.

Well, there were three possibilities: the cemetery, Allison's house, or the attorney's office. Sadly, I couldn't be in three places at once. The attorney's office was too early, but either of the other two were possibilities.

"Sir, would you like a taxi?"

"No. You have a rental car office on site?"

"Yes, but it doesn't open for another two hours."

"Shit!"

Three guests walked in then, all men dressed in business suits looking like they were going to a meeting.

"Sir," the front office manager said, taking me aside. "You need a vehicle to rent?"

"Yes."

"I'll get the paperwork filled out and we'll put the

charges on the card you left for the room. You can get your car and take care of your business."

"Thank you. I appreciate it."

I guessed he wanted to get me out of there. Well, that was fine by me. I followed him to the counter, filled out as much of the paperwork as was absolutely required, took the keys, and found my car: a fucking Ford Taurus.

"Nothing faster?" I asked him.

"No, sir, I'm afraid not."

"All right. Thank you."

I left, peeling out of the lot more quickly than they probably liked, and headed in the direction of the cemetery. I hoped it was early enough that there wouldn't be many visitors. I knew the address, but the lot was quite large and I didn't know the plot of land where Mia's sister's memorial was. I hoped the taxi driver at least drove more slowly than I did, buying me a little time.

Arriving at the cemetery, I saw several taxis as I navigated the lanes — but none of them contained Mia. I followed the road through the entire place, but about a half hour in, I decided this was like searching for a needle in a haystack and drove back out.

That was when I finally spotted her climbing into a cab.

I slowed the car, putting the sun visor down in the hopes she wouldn't see me. She carried the backpack and looked to be drying her eyes. The taxi drove slowly out of the cemetery and I followed, more relieved than I had imagined I would be. She was so naïve to do this on her own. What the hell had she been thinking? Especially after my confession of the night before.

But maybe that was just it. Maybe in her mind, she was keeping me safe from them by going alone.

Christ. Once we got through this, I was going to spank

that little ass of hers and I was going to enjoy every second of it.

I knew where she was headed. She was going to see Allison. I still wasn't convinced of Allison's motives but had a feeling the one who'd ratted us out to Samuel St. Rose was the same person who'd sent the assassins after us in that little village. I didn't trust her. She was a St. Rose, and blood was blood.

Allison lived in Germantown, a posh neighborhood on the outskirts of Philadelphia. I parked down the street and watched as the taxi came to a stop and Mia climbed out, saying something to the man. The taxi waited there for her as she walked up toward the front porch and rang the doorbell. Allison answered within a few minutes and although I was too far to see facial expressions, I did see Allison pull her in for a big hug. Soon though, they appeared to argue about something before Mia walked back to the taxi, slipped some bills to the man from the window and let him go. So, they'd been arguing about that. Well, Allison seemed to have won that one.

I settled in to my uncomfortable rental and decided to wait. It wasn't long before I knew just whose side Allison was on.

26

MIA

*I*t was good to see Allison again. I'd made the right decision to come here. I could trust her; she was on my side.

I told her about Julien, leaving out the part about him being a hit man, the part about Samuel having hired him. Told her about Italy, and Gianna, and how I hoped to go back there once this was all over.

"How are things here? With Samuel, I mean?"

"I don't talk to him much." She poured another cup of tea for both of us. "It's pretty much business as usual for him, I guess. You know I stay out of that."

"I know. And it's smart. What about Jason?"

God, did I even want to know? Even hearing myself say that name aloud sent shivers through me.

"Jason is... Jason."

That scared me.

"He thinks you owe him, and as far as he's concerned, you broke your promise to keep silent — so that million doesn't belong to you."

"What do you think?"

She shrugged and turned her attention to stirring sugar into her tea. "What he did was wrong. But I also don't agree with how my father and Tanya handled it." She only met my gaze again once she was through, the look in her eyes strange, different than I'd expected. The warmth was gone.

"How about the way I handled it? Do you think what I did was wrong?"

"I didn't say that. What happened to you shouldn't have happened." Allison checked her watch. "Let me go have a shower and get dressed. Then we'll go. You sure you're not hungry?"

Allison was going to take me to the attorney's office. I liked the idea of having her there with me in case any other members of her family showed up. "No, I'm fine. I'm anxious to get this done."

"Okay. I'll be quick."

She went upstairs to her bedroom and I poured myself another cup of tea. Julien would be up by now and he'd see that I was gone. If today went well and I managed to get that money transferred to my account, I'd find a way to pay him what I promised to pay.

I got up to use the bathroom, but just as I did, I heard the sound of a car door closing. I knew instantly that something was wrong. I went to the window by the front door and saw a car parked at the end of Allison's driveway. The shower switched off upstairs at the same moment I heard a key slip into the lock of the back door. I just watched as if it were all happening in slow motion, as Jason and a man I didn't know walked into the house. Jason's eyes trained upon me, the malevolence in his gaze seeming to physically push me deeper into the corner my back already pressed against.

"Well, well, well," he said, the other man closing the door behind them. "Look what the cat dragged in?"

"Jason."

Allison came down the stairs dressed in jeans and a t-shirt, drying her hair with a towel. She looked at them, then at me. She seemed so casual, so relaxed... and I knew from the expression on her face that she'd been the one to call Jason, to tell him I was here.

"Allison?" I didn't take my eyes off Jason as I spoke to her.

He'd changed. A lot. He'd gotten older, bigger, meaner. And in his black eyes, all I saw was hate.

"Allison's got nothing to do with this, Mia. This is between you and me." Jason approached then, coming to stand just inches from me, his towering form making me feel like I had when I was thirteen.

When he'd raped and beaten me.

"Jason, you said you only wanted to talk," Allison said.

I realized it wasn't only my hands shaking then. Being near him had always scared the shit out of me, but now, now that it was just me and him, his goon and Allison? I was terrified.

Jason looked me over from head to toe. "Life treating you well, Mia?" His hand closed over my arm.

I screamed and Allison grabbed hold of him, trying to pull him off. "You promised you wouldn't hurt her!"

"You told him I was here?" I couldn't believe what I was hearing.

Jason's goon was on Allison in an instant, easily taking her away, holding her just a few feet from us, all while Jason's eyes bored into mine.

"Jason, whatever you think you're doing—"

"Shut the fuck up, cunt. You owe me. You put me behind bars, Mia, when you'd made a promise."

"Jason, don't!" It was Allison again but he wasn't listening to her anymore.

"Take my sister upstairs," Jason told the goon.

"No!" Allison yelled, but the man easily lifted her off her feet, carrying her struggling form to the stairs. "Mia, he promised he only wanted to talk!"

"Don't believe her, Mia. She let me trace the last call you made too. That's how I found out where you were." Jason stepped even closer, pressing himself against me, the feel of him sickening me. "Back for the money? You think it's yours?"

"Get away from me, Jason."

Gripping both of my arms, he dragged me into the study, kicking the door closed behind us.

"Answer the fucking question, whore."

"Let me go!" He pushed me against the wall, his gaze scanning the length of me, the look in his eyes coupled with the way he licked his lips terrifying. "Please, Jason, let me go."

"I guess since you told anyway, I got a little something owed to me. Hell, I'd even give you the money. But your pussy sure ain't worth a million bucks. Now, your sister—"

With a strength I didn't now I had, I raised my hands up to his face and clawed my nails down his cheeks, wanting to scratch out his eyes for what he'd done to Tanya. To me. "I wasn't enough? You fucking asshole. You had to rape her too? She was your father's wife!"

He drew his fist back and punched me so hard in my stomach that I doubled over, all the breath pushed out of me. When he let me go, I slid to the floor. I watched him wipe at his face, saw the streaks of blood.

"Bitch, you'll pay for that!" He grabbed me again and I screamed as loud as I could. Just as he shoved me over the desk, the door smashed open and there stood Julien, pissed as fuck, his weapon in hand.

He shot first, the popping sound different in real life than it was in the movies. Jason cursed and fell backward. Julien advanced on him, his face red with anger, and aimed again.

"Julien, don't! He's not worth it!"

"I don't know, Mia. Feels pretty damn good to me." He fired again, the bullet striking Jason in the thigh. A patch of blood spread on the shoulder of Jason's white dress shirt, probably from the first bullet, and his face creased with pain. Before I could warn Julien, the hulking form of Jason's goon filled the doorway, another shot ringing out, this one catching Julien's arm just as he swung around to face the intruder.

"Kill him, but I want *her* alive!" Jason ordered.

Julien had stumbled but was still standing when the man aimed at him again.

"Where the fuck do you idiots learn to shoot?" Julien muttered, moving so fast I barely saw him raise his arm before hearing the shot, sending the goon's huge body crashing to the floor, his pistol clattering to the ground as his body crumpled in the too small room, half in and half out of the doorway.

"Mia!" Allison's tear-streaked face turned up at the door and Julien trained his weapon on her. I ran to him, creating a barrier between him and her.

"Don't, Julien. Please!"

"She called him here, Mia. Get the fuck out of the way."

"No!"

It was in that moment that Jason lunged forward, a

blade in his hand. I screamed and Julien shoved me out of the way, and, at the same time, fired off one more shot, sending Jason sprawling on his back.

"Stay the fuck down!" Julien barked.

Jason wasn't dead, but from the look on his face, he was in agonizing pain. Julien had shot his other arm.

I looked at him down there on the floor, then turned to find Allison crying at the door. Julien straightened himself up and came to me. "You hurt?"

I shook my head. "It's okay, nothing bad."

"Why the fuck would you think it was a good idea to do this on your own?"

I opened my mouth to answer, but he held up his hand.

"Never mind. Where's the backpack?"

"Inside."

"Let's go."

Allison cleared the way when we approached, letting him pass, touching my arm as I went by. "I'm sorry, Mia. I promise I didn't know he'd hurt you."

I looked at her, but I couldn't forgive her. She knew what he'd done to me, and yet, she'd betrayed me in the end. If it weren't for Julien, God knows what Jason would be doing to me right now.

Julien checked inside the backpack, confirmed the ledger was there and turned to me. "Let's go, Mia."

"Please, Mia. I'm sorry," Allison said.

"I can't look at you, Allison." I walked toward Julien who seemed in a rush to get out of there. And I knew why as soon as we reached the front door because it opened just as he reached for the doorknob... and there stood Samuel St. Rose along with two bodyguards. He likely had even more outside.

Samuel surveyed the scene while Julien and I stood

there. He craned his head around us to see his son in the next room before stepping deeper into the house along with the two bodyguards. One of them closed the front door.

"Mia," Samuel said, looking me over from head to toe. "God, the resemblance is incredible. You look so much like your sister."

I stared up at him, unable to speak, my heart racing in my chest, my hand trembling in Julien's.

"You must be Julien."

Julien nodded. "I am."

"Drop your weapon, Julien."

Julien glanced at the two men whose pistols were tucked into the waistbands of their pants, and did as he was told, his pistol clattering to the floor.

Samuel smiled. "Well, delivery of the girl we've got. Where's the book?"

Julien held up the backpack and I looked at him. What was he doing? Was he going to just hand me over? Leave me here in this house of lunatics?

Samuel gestured to one of the guards who took the bag and opened it. "It's here, boss."

"Any copies?" Samuel asked both of us.

"No," Julien lied.

Samuel studied him, his eyes cold. "Then you've earned your money. But"—he touched the downed goon with the toe of one shoe and looked at his son—"you've left a mess."

"Couldn't be helped," Julien said casually, holding not my hand, but my arm now, the grip of his fingers a remorseless clamp around my flesh.

Samuel turned his attention to his daughter. "Allison, go to your room."

"This is my house."

"That I paid for. Go the fuck to your room."

I'd never heard him talk like that to her before.

"No."

His eyes turned to stone and I could feel Allison tremble beside me. "He was going to hurt her. Like he did before. Like he did Tanya."

I watched Samuel's face all along, and when she said that last part, his lips tightened, his hands fisting at his sides.

"Well, now that you've arranged for this family reunion, I will take care of things with Jason. But I don't need you around to watch. Go. Upstairs."

Allison looked at me once. "Don't kill her in the house."

My mouth fell open and a chill gripped me. Without even the tiniest flicker of emotion in her eyes, she climbed the stairs up to the second floor.

Once we heard the door close behind her, I turned to Samuel who only raised his eyebrows at me, as if to say he knew, as if to say how stupid I was to be surprised. He then stepped over the lifeless body of the man Julien had killed and walked toward his son.

For the first time, I saw fear in Jason's eyes.

"Been a long time, boy." Samuel squatted down to look at the damage Julien had done but continued to speak, this time, addressing me. "Haven't seen this piece of shit since he got out of prison." He looked down at his son. "Did you think I wouldn't find out what you did to her?" He pulled a pistol from inside his suit jacket and brought it to Jason's chin. "She was my wife." His voice was tight.

"She was a whore, father. A fucking prostitute."

Samuel drew in a long breath and Julien's grip on my arm tightened.

"I should never have covered up for you the first time. Maybe if I hadn't, Tanya would be here now instead of you, you worthless son of a bitch."

Samuel cocked the pistol. Jason's eyes went wide as he looked from the gun, to his father's face.

"She came when I fucked her. Twice. *Your wife* came with my cock in her cunt."

"I saw the video, Jason. You're a rapist. I should have taken care of you the first time around, but I wanted to give you another chance. Look what it cost me." He brought the gun to Jason's mouth. "Open up, boy. Time to say goodbye."

I couldn't believe what I was seeing. He was going to kill his own son. Right here in cold blood.

Jason's eyes had widened and he tried to turn his face away, but Samuel held it, squeezing his jaw, forcing his mouth open to push the barrel of the gun inside. He held it there and even I couldn't stand the terror on Jason's face. I felt nothing but contempt for him, but this was too much.

Samuel chuckled once and I followed his gaze to Jason's pants where a dark patch spread at the crotch. "You pissin' yourself, boy?" Samuel's grin turned evil. "What's the matter? You only the big man when you can hold down girls half your size so you can fuck them?"

Jason tried to say something but the pistol made a jumble out of the words. Even so, I knew he was begging. It only seemed to piss Samuel off more though and he thrust the gun painfully farther into Jason's mouth.

"Samuel, don't do it." I couldn't watch this. I didn't want this.

Samuel half turned to me, the look on his face one of annoyance. "Can you believe it? She should be the one to put the bullet in your head and she's telling me to stop." Samuel addressed the next part of the question to me. "You know he raped your sister?"

I nodded. "I know. That's why she stole the ledger and

ran. She was scared of him. He threatened her that he was going to tell you she seduced him."

A quick moment of emotion flashed across Samuel's eyes, but it was gone as quickly as it came. "She should have come to me, not run away. I had fucking video cameras everywhere. She knew that."

"Well, maybe given what happened in the past she wasn't so sure what you'd do, Samuel." I knew I was taking a chance, but I couldn't just back down. I couldn't tuck my tail between my legs and say yes again. He'd bullied me into shutting up when it happened to me, but now, my sister was dead. "That's why she took the ledger. Jason threatened to harm her, to go to you, but he also told her he'd come after me again. I know she felt responsible for what happened to me. That and guilt at how it was covered up."

Samuel pulled the gun from Jason's mouth and slowly stood.

"Stop, Mia," Julien's voice came steady and strong in my ear.

"No. I shut up about it the first time and look what happened."

Samuel walked toward me. "I loved Tanya."

I nodded, tears in my eyes. "I know. But that didn't help her, did it?"

"Mia." It was Julien again, but I kept my gaze steady on Samuel's. Whatever happened now would happen, but this needed to be said.

"No, it did not," Samuel agreed, putting his weapon back into his coat. "Load that piece of shit into the trunk," he said to the men who'd entered with him. "I'll deal with him later." "Confirm for me there are no copies of that ledger, Mia," he said, stepping closer to me, his body a physical threat. Even though Julien was bigger, there were three of them and one of Julien and they all still had their weapons.

"There are no copies, Samuel." It took all I had to keep my voice steady, to not cower away. I had to remember that this man was once kind to me, that he loved my sister, and that somehow, she loved him. "I don't mean you any harm. I just want to live my life quietly."

He nodded once, then turned to Julien. "Delivery was for both the girl and the ledger. Since you only brought me the ledger, you don't get paid."

"Fine." Julien's voice didn't falter once. He was like a solid rock by my side.

"You will have no more contact from my family. The money your sister left you is yours. Collect it and disappear, Mia."

My heart raced. Was I hearing correctly? The guards stepped aside once Samuel gestured for them to do so.

"Let's go," Julien said, tugging at my arm when I didn't move. But when he bent to pick up his weapon, Samuel covered it with his shoe.

"Leave it."

Julien nodded once and we walked to the door, his hand around my arm holding me tight to him. The guard opened the door and we stepped out. That was when I heard Allison calling out from the stairs.

"Mia!"

I looked over my shoulder, but Julien yanked at my arm. "We need to go. Now."

"He's my brother, Mia. What did you expect me to do? Choose you over him?"

I met Allison's gaze, disgusted with what I saw there, then turned away. I was finished with the St. Roses. We walked across the lawn, Julien not once letting me go until we reached what I assumed was his rental car. He opened the passenger side, put me in my seat and closed the door. He then walked around the car to the driver's side and climbed inside. I looked at him, and he at me. Then, without a word, he reached over and pulled the seatbelt across my chest, buckling me in.

"Ready?"

I nodded. He started the car and we drove out of that street. I didn't look back but noticed Julien watching in the rearview mirror until we turned the corner. We were silent until he merged onto the highway that would take us back into the city.

I watched him drive, taking in his features, the hard line of his jaw, the intensity in his eyes as he checked the rearview mirror every few moments. "I'm sorry you didn't get paid."

He glanced at me quickly. "Don't worry about it." He focused on the road again.

"Are we going to the attorney?"

"Yes, then you're going to disappear, like Samuel said."

He seemed angry as he spoke the words.

"Thank you for following me and... saving me. I don't know what Jason would have done —"

"You don't?" he asked.

Yep, he was pissed.

"I—"

"He would have raped you first, then probably put a bullet in your head."

"I didn't want to involve anyone else. I didn't want you to get hurt too."

"I can take care of myself, Mia. Although I did lose a brand new revolver."

"I'm going to pay you what I promised. You can... buy a new one, I guess?"

He checked his phone against the street name and made a turn. The attorney's office wasn't too far. "You're going to need to keep that money and stay gone after this, Mia. I don't trust Samuel St. Rose or his family."

"No, I'm going to pay you."

We parked the car outside the office building and Julien shut off the engine before turning to me. "No, you're going to do exactly as you're told for once in your life. And just so we're clear, you're getting your ass whipped for running off like you did. You could have been killed, Mia. Dead. You get it?"

I nodded. "I do. Thank you."

"Let's go."

27

JULIEN

*T*he attorney knew we were coming. Hell, he had the paperwork ready to go and seemed more than a little anxious to get us out of there. I stayed with Mia while she signed off on several forms, and within fifteen minutes, she was given access information to a bank account already set up in her name with the money sitting there just as promised.

Now, to figure out how to get her gone and make her stay gone.

I didn't trust Samuel St. Rose and I trusted Allison even less. I had a feeling he was going to take care of Jason, which was fine by me. Saved me some work. But Allison was another story. And on top of everything, I had my own shit to figure out. Cash was going to be pissed, as was Ryan. But when Mia slipped her hand into mine as soon as we were out of the attorney's office, I knew I'd have to deal with all of that later. There was something more important to think about now.

We rode down on the elevator without speaking, but I kept her hand in mine. My phone rang once we were out on the street and I looked at the display. It was Cash. Declining the call, I slipped the phone back into my pocket and took out the pack of cigarettes. I hadn't smoked in a few days. Hadn't even thought about it actually. I went to take one out, but stopped. Mia watched me as I tossed the pack into a nearby trashcan. She smiled.

"I can't believe it's over," she said as I unlocked the car.

"Well, it's not really over until you transfer that money out to another account the St. Roses don't have anything to do with. Then you get yourself gone."

"You think he'd take it back? Why would he?"

I shrugged a shoulder as I cut across two lanes to make our turn. "I don't know. Because he's a criminal? I wouldn't trust him, Mia. He put a gun into his own son's mouth. Remember that."

Mia shivered. "You were right about Allison. I'm sorry I didn't listen to you."

"That was forgiven. You know that."

"What now, Julien? I mean, what happens after we do all of that. Transfer the money out and *get me gone*?"

"You live your life like you wanted to, without having to look over your shoulder."

I felt her eyes on me as I pulled into the circular drive of the hotel's front entrance and parked the car. Only once I pulled the keys out of the ignition did I stop to look at her and saw the questions in her eyes.

"You can go anywhere, Mia. Start fresh. Be anything, do anything."

"What about you?"

"What about me?" I chuckled but my chest tightened at her words, at the way she said them, like that lost little girl again. "I'm no good. A mercenary, Mia. A hitman. It's what

I've been doing for a very long time. People like me don't get second chances."

"No, you *are* good, Julien. You helped me when you didn't have to. When you could have gained more if you hadn't."

I smiled at her sweetness, her innocence. "You have a chance to start again. Seems silly if you don't take it after all that's happened."

"I promised your grandmother I'd be back."

I rubbed my hand along the back of my neck. "She'll understand." Mia was stalling and I wasn't sure I wanted her to say what she was afraid to say.

"What about what you said last night?"

But there it was. I took a deep breath, then another. The valet chose that moment to open my door and we both looked up at him.

"Let's go in, Mia."

She studied me for a moment before nodding and climbing out of the car. She stood patiently by as I handed in the key for the rental car and we rode the elevator up in silence, even though the air around us was so thick you could slice it with a knife.

"Julien?" she said, taking hold of my hand once the elevator doors opened and I climbed out. "You said some things last night and I want to know if they were true — or if you were just saying whatever you thought you needed to say to make me stay."

A hotel room door opened and a couple walked out into the hallway, mid-argument from the sound of it. They were so involved in themselves that they barely noticed us.

"Let's go, Mia."

We went to our room where she sat on the edge of the

bed. "Did you lie? Make that stuff up so you could keep control of me?"

I shook my head. "No, I meant everything I said. Besides, I didn't exactly keep control of you, did I?"

"Why do I get the feeling I will never see you again once we leave this hotel?"

"Because you won't."

Mia slumped back as if I'd struck her, and the look of betrayal on her face wounded me. I sat down next to her. "Mia," I took her face in my hands and forced her to look at me. Her eyes were wide and red with unspent tears she tried desperately to keep from falling. "The fact that I care about you is enough of a reason for us not to be together. There are people who will always be looking for me. It's a part of the business I'm in. On my own, I'm less vulnerable. And just so you know, the people I'm talking about, they would hurt you if it meant they could get to me."

"So I'm a liability."

"Christ. No, you're not a liability. I can take care of myself. I just couldn't stand it if something happened to you, Mia. If something happened to you because of me, because of *my line of work*, as you once put it."

"You could stop. I have a million dollars, half of which rightfully is yours. We made a deal and you kept your end of the bargain. I plan to keep mine."

She looked so hopeful, but I could see my reflection in her eyes. My face already said what I needed to put to words. "It's not that easy."

"I don't care. I have feelings for you too, Julien. And it's more than caring about you or having you under my skin. I think I love you. No, I *know* I do. And I don't want to spend one minute away from you."

Now I was the one who was shocked for the first time in

my life. "You don't mean that, Mia. This is just leftover from what we've been through together over the last weeks. What happened was intense, and you came to rely on me for your survival. I made it that way, made you need me. You should hate me, Mia. I would understand if you hated me."

"I don't hate you. I will never hate you, and you're wrong. Besides, if you meant what you said last night, does that mean you can feel it but I can't?"

"That's not what I said."

"It's exactly what you said." She stood and paced. "I mean, it's true, you never said the words you loved me, but I think—"

I stood and pulled her to me. "Woman, you push all my buttons!"

She opened her mouth to speak but I crushed mine over hers just to shut her up. "You want me?"

"Yes!"

"You want this?" I pushed her down onto the bed and whipped my belt off. "This is what you get with me, Mia." Her eyes went wide as I straddled her, taking both her wrists and wrapping my belt around them before running it through the rungs of the headboard. "Remember how I said I owed you an ass whipping?"

I wanted to scare her and from the look in her eyes, it was working. I didn't like it, but I had to do it. This romance — it was a joke. A fucking joke. She could never have a life with me and even though I may have entertained the idea for a minute, I couldn't do it to her. I had to get my head out of my ass and do the right thing.

"Julien—"

I undid her belt and yanked it out of its loops, then unbuttoned her jeans and flipped her onto her belly, tugging her pants and panties down to her knees. "This is who I am." I stood and doubled her belt over, gripping the buckle. It was thinner than mine, but would do the job. Striking once, I watched as the thin welt formed instantly. "This is what you get with me." I struck again, twice in quick succession, "You get your ass whipped for disobedience. Every time." She pulled at her restraints but remained lying there, taking it, a small cry following each of the strokes as she bit down on her lip to try to remain silent. "You get to hide all your life long and we both know you're not very good at that."

"I don't care!"

"You don't get to have a home." I striped her bottom as I spoke, but avoided marking her thighs.

"I said I don't care!"

"You need to know what you're asking for. See who I am, rather than who you've made me out to be." I struck without speaking then, just laid stroke after stroke down on her ass. Mia lay there taking it, not fighting me, not resisting. After a few moments, she climbed up onto her knees and offered her ass to me, to the belt, and I punished her with it, knowing even though I tried to push her away, even though I knew that was the right thing to do, some part of me hoped she'd choose me anyway. Hoped she'd want me to stay.

Because I would have her. I would change everything for her.

"Julien."

I stopped when she called out my name, and when her gaze met mine, I felt the heat of tears, of everything I was trying to hold inside of me surface in my eyes. I turned away from her, stepping back from the bed. It took me a minute, but I looked at what I'd done, looked at her red, welted ass, looked at her eyes, those green depths bright, her lashes wet.

Dropping the belt, I sat down on the bed and unbound her wrists. She rolled onto her side and sat up. She was so close, I could feel the heat from her body before she set her face against mine.

"Julien."

"This is who I am, Mia." I couldn't look at her. "Everyone I love gets hurt eventually. Everyone. It's never not happened."

She turned my face to meet her gaze, her little hands holding me so I couldn't look away. I didn't want to look away, but I wasn't strong enough to do it alone.

"Do you mean that?"

"What?"

"You love me?"

I stared at her, taking her hands in one of mine and pushing the hair that had stuck to her face back behind her ear. "You're so pretty, Mia. I don't even think you know it." I kissed her lips softly, before moving to kiss the tip of her nose, and then her forehead. I inhaled deeply, taking in the scent of her, memorizing it.

"I don't even know your last name," she said. "Your real last name."

"DeAngelo."

"Julien DeAngelo." She nodded her head as if it all made sense now. She pulled back to look at me. "I want you exactly as you are. I don't care what you've done. I don't care about anything. I want to go back to Pitigliano with you. And I want to start fresh there. With you."

"With me?"

She nodded. "Say it, Julien. Say the words."

I took her face in my hands, wiping away a single tear with my thumb. "I love you, Mia. I love you."

EPILOGUE ONE

MIA

The first six months were difficult. Julien disappeared twice, leaving me at the house on my own for a week at a time during each occasion. I never did find out where he went. He didn't talk about it, and I didn't ask.

When Gianna saw us walk into the café hand in hand when we'd returned to Italy, I could almost physically feel her relief. She had been shocked to see us, and when she'd hugged both me and Julien, she'd spoken so fast I hadn't understood a word she'd said, but her face had been wet with tears she'd tried hard to conceal.

Julien had been quiet, but we were doing the right thing. He belonged here and it was time to make up for lost years. I gave Julien and his grandmother space, but I never felt left out when it was the three of us. In a way, I felt that I was a sort of safe haven for Julien. A place he could rest when memories and the thoughts of all that had been taken from him, taken from all of them, overwhelmed. In time, I hoped some of those memories would be fond remembrances rather than painful reminders, but he didn't talk much about that part of things. I knew it was difficult for him and resigned myself to being there when he was ready — and for those times he wasn't, I'd be there to comfort him however I could.

Now that I had no more ties to the St. Rose family, I felt free. I forgave Tanya for what I'd thought were her sins. In a way, I'd known all along she had been doing what she thought best. I realized during the time of the cover-up that she was young and Samuel was a much older, very dominant man. He had loved her, but standing up to him was almost impossible for her. It always had been now that I thought of their relationship. It was just that most of the time, there wasn't any need to. He'd tried to please her and make her happy, but in that instance, he'd chosen wrong. Too bad that choice had had such terrible and final consequences.

But that was the past. I was determined to live in the present.

"Cake is ready!" I said.

Gianna came into the kitchen. "Oh! It's perfect!" She swiped her thumb over the edge of the plate, pretending to clean it, but truly wanting to taste the frosting. It was Julien's favorite cake, supposedly. Gianna had dug up the recipe and I'd baked it. A simple yellow cake with dark chocolate icing from his great-great grandmother's days.

"Gianna?" I gave her a chastising look, but it was funny to see this sixty-something woman stand there sucking frosting off her finger.

"Just want to make sure it is right." She picked up the candles I'd insisted on. It was Julien's birthday. He was turning thirty, and we were surprising him. Neither of us were sure if he'd like the idea but we didn't care. He needed to have some fun. We all did. Only problem was, he'd left early this morning without a word and I knew Gianna was as anxious as I to see him return. We had more than enough money to live on, he didn't need to do any more jobs, and I wanted him to stop. Even though I'd told him I could accept him as he was, I wanted that part of his life to end.

At half past seven that night, I left the café to get changed. We'd decorated and were expecting guests at eight. I took the longer route by the cemetery to the house, but he wasn't there — and he wasn't at the house either. I had a quick shower and changed, forcing myself not to worry. The last two times he'd left, he'd told me he was going. I hadn't pushed for details. I knew when not to. I just hoped the pattern hadn't changed to where he'd just leave without a word. Things were so uncertain with him. I wondered if they would always be.

At eight o'clock, I made my way to the café, but I felt a little deflated. Gianna smiled at me when I arrived but she couldn't hide her disappointment when I walked in alone. Several guests had already arrived, the old men taking their usual places while the women collected around the tables that had been pushed together to make one long one. Everyone wanted to help and people were in good spirits, eating and drinking. But all I could do was wait.

Shortly after I arrived, Angela walked into the café. I hadn't seen her since that day at the shop. I had purposely been avoiding her, and now I wasn't really sure why. I trusted Julien, but for some reason, I felt protective of him when she was around, even though he didn't pay her a moment's attention.

"Where is the birthday boy?" she asked, pouring herself a glass of wine.

"Running an errand."

"Hmm. He's been gone all day, hasn't he?"

I faced her. "Are you trying to say something, Angela?"

She gave me an innocent look. "Me? No. Just making an observation."

"When do you go back to Rome?" I asked.

Gianna joined us, her own drink in hand. "Yes, Angela, when do you leave?"

I almost spit my drink out at the way she said it.

"Three months," Angela said, gloating. "I dropped my summer course so I could help my grandmother."

"So selfless of you," Gianna commented.

I checked my watch and I could see from the corner of my eye Angela open her mouth, but before she could speak, Julien entered, stopping short when he saw everyone, saw how the café had been decorated.

"Surprise!" Gianna and I yelled, although we were probably the most surprised out of everyone there. I exhaled a long breath when he entered and though it took him a moment, he finally smiled.

"What's all this?"

"Your birthday," Gianna said, intercepting him on his way to me. "Happy birthday, Julien." She sounded like she'd wanted to say that for years. I saw her push an envelope into his hand before she turned for the kitchen.

Julien looked at it, then stuffed it into his pocket unopened and came to hug me. "Is this your doing?"

"Mine and your grandmother's. Happy birthday."

He kissed me, our foreheads touching as he did.

"I don't have anything for you—" I said.

"I have everything I need right here," he said, wrapping his arms around me.

I smiled up at him, wanting to ask where he'd been but not wanting to spoil this moment, knowing I had to take him as I could get him.

"Happy birthday, Julien," Angela said, opening her arms to hug him. She was unbelievable.

Julien looked at her as if seeing her there for the first time. "Oh. Thank you, Angela. Where's your grandmother? I promised to come by and help put some shelving together for her."

Angela grinned and sent a sly look my way. "Well, I'm taking care of the shop for the summer and I'll be there all day tomorrow. Why don't you come by then?"

He nodded, peeling her hand off his arm. "I'll talk to Myra later."

The lights went out and Gianna came out of the kitchen carrying the cake, all thirty candles burning bright. Julien took my hand and held it, and I knew he felt a little uncomfortable with all the attention. He was a man used to being invisible. Everyone joined in to sing.

"We never celebrated your birthday properly, Mia," he whispered to me.

"I am more than okay to forget this particular birthday."

He smiled but when it was time to blow out the candles, he tugged on my hand. I leaned down with him and we blew them out together. He kissed my cheek. "I have something for you."

"For me?"

"Mia baked it, Julien," Gianna interrupted, setting a huge slice onto a plate and handing it to him. "See what you think."

He took the fork and scooped up a giant mouthful. His lips stretched into a grin and he nodded, shoving a second forkful in before putting the cake down. I wiped the frosting from the corner of his mouth and he smiled.

"My favorite. And it's just like I remember."

It was so strange but I felt so very proud in that moment

and he must have seen it on my face, in my huge smile. Gianna served the cake out and Julien took my hand and led me into the kitchen.

"I don't think we should leave your party. You're the guest of honor!"

"Shh," he said, looking into the café from the opening between the kitchen and the counter before pushing me to a corner where we wouldn't be seen. There, he pressed me against the wall with his body and kissed me like a man starving. "I love how you taste, how you smell. I love every-thing about you, Mia."

He looked down at me and I smoothed my hands over his shoulders, feeling his muscles beneath the tight-fitting shirt. "I wasn't sure if you were coming home today."

I said it before I could stop myself. I knew he cared about me, and I wanted to make things easy for him, but I needed him to know my fears too.

He grew serious. "I understand. And I know it's not been easy for you, with me I mean. I know I can be distant at times. Believe it or not, I do feel better, in a way. It's good to be home again."

"I'm glad, Julien."

"You've been more than patient with me and I want you to know something. I'll never simply leave here, leave you, without a word again. Ever."

I nodded, but was it enough? Would it ever be enough as long as he did what he did?

"I had to take care of something in Cortona today," he said, reaching into his pocket and pulling out a small box. "Took longer than I expected."

I'd always heard the saying 'my heart skipped a beat' but I'd never felt it until that moment.

But his smile disappeared and his face grew serious

again. "Mia, I'm done with Cash. With the past. I know that's a reason you worried I wouldn't come back today, but I want you to know that's never going to happen again. I'm here to stay." He went down on one knee then, fumbled with the box for a moment and for the first time since I'd known Julien, I saw that he was nervous. Even when men shot guns at him, I'd not seen him falter. It was strange and endearing, in a way.

Finally, he got the box open and turned it to me, his eyes glistening when I met them after glimpsing the old-fashioned gold band in the box, the diamond glittering on top of it.

"It was my mother's. I had to have it resized for you and the jeweler who made it for them lives in Cortona."

"Julien—"

"I love you, Mia, and I want you to marry me. I want you to be my wife, and I want to spend the rest of my life with you."

My hand trembled as I went to touch the ring.

"Will you marry me, Mia?"

A warm tear streaked down my face and I sniffled, meeting his tear-filled eyes. Unable to speak, I nodded, covering my mouth when he stood and took the ring from the box. Without a word, he slipped it onto my finger, the fit perfect.

"It looks beautiful," he said.

I looked up to meet his gaze and he kissed my cheek, kissed the tear there.

"Don't cry, Mia. We've had too many tears. It's time to laugh."

I smiled. "I'm happy, Julien. These are *not* sad tears."

The door opened just as he went to kiss me and Gianna came in, carrying the cake plate with one remaining piece on it. The moment she saw us she stopped —and would have backed out if Julien hadn't called her over.

"You'll be the first to know, Gran," he said, holding my hand up.

Her eyes reddened instantly. "It was your mother's."

Julien nodded and Gianna cried, taking us both into her embrace at once, kissing us, and again, talking too fast for me to understand.

"Did you open the envelope?" she asked him when she stepped back.

Julien looked confused for a moment but then reached into his pocket and took out a folded envelope.

Gianna shook her head and took it from his hand, straightening it out. She handed it back to him with a soft smack against the side of his head, and he opened it, pulling out an official looking form. While he read it, I looked at it over his shoulder.

"You're giving me the café?"

"I'm giving it to both of you. And I hope you'll give it to your children one day."

I felt Julien's gaze shift to me, but I kept mine on Gianna. I was happy, I wasn't going to think about what couldn't be right now. And who knew, the doctor didn't say it would be impossible. He'd said it would be a miracle.

"I want you to stay, Julien. Now that you're home, I want you to stay."

"So you're buying me?" he teased.

"Whatever it takes. Besides"—she wrapped an arm over my shoulder—"I need this one here. If you two leave now, I don't know what I'll do short of following you wherever you go. You probably don't want that."

We all chuckled. "We're staying Gran." He turned to me. "We're staying."

EPILOGUE TWO

JULIEN

I'd seen Mia's face when Gran had mentioned children. She tried to hide her sadness about the fact that she'd be unlikely to have any, but she couldn't hide it from me.

Well, nothing was impossible and I'd do my part to keep trying, that was for sure. Even if it didn't work, we still had options. Adoption was something I'd be very interested in. In a way, I thought of it as a way of paying it back for Charlie, saving another kid from what happened to him. Was I seeking redemption for my own sins? I didn't know, and I didn't care.

"Ready to go?" I asked as the last of the dishes were dried and put away. It was close to midnight and everyone had finally left. We'd sent Gran home to bed and Mia and I had cleaned up our café.

"Yep. I'm exhausted!"

"Well, owning a café will likely do that to you."

She smiled and slipped off the apron she'd been wearing. I took her hand, pulling her to me, kissing her, feeling the sharp edge of the ring she wore, the ring that promised she'd be mine, in the palm of my hand. Sliding my hand down her back to cup her soft little bottom, I hoisted her up and carried her to the counter, never breaking off our kiss as I set her there, pushing her dress up to her waist before opening the buttons at the front and taking out her breasts. She'd worn a bra, and the little mounds fit perfectly in my palms, the nipples hardening instantly.

"Julien, what are you doing?"

She asked it through a kiss and I grinned, reaching my head down to suck one breast into my mouth before drawing the nipple out between my teeth. Her hands on my shoulders squeezed and she groaned. Sliding one hand down between her legs, I slipped it into her panties as I took her other breast into my mouth, sucking and tasting, concentrating on that nipple as moisture collected on my fingers. Straightening again, I kissed her, lifting her slightly as I did to drag her panties off. I then knelt, pulling her to the very edge of the counter as she leaned her head back against the wall and opened her legs.

"I love how you smell." I couldn't get enough of it, actually. When she was aroused, it was like a call to me, and I loved that I did that to her.

Gripping her hips, I took her clit into my mouth, making her moan instantly as I began to suck softly. Her hands closed around my head and she pulled me to her so my face pressed into her pussy as she leaned back some more, setting her feet up on the counter and spreading her legs wider. Her clit swelled in my mouth and I knew she was close from the sounds she was making so I slowed, looking up at her face before pulling back and standing, looking at her sex, at the gaping lips of her pussy, her slick, pink cunt.

"Julien—"

Pulling off my shirt, I gripped a handful of hair and tugged her head backward, looking down at her face, her open mouth. I kissed her, letting her taste herself on my tongue while she worked the zipper of my jeans, opening them and pushing them down to free my swollen cock. Lifting her up off the counter, I pushed her to her knees where she greedily opened her mouth and took me in.

Christ, she was so fucking good. Her hair tangled in my fingers, and I worked her over my length, pushing deeper, watching her as I did, loving the feel of that hot little mouth, that wet tongue working while she watched me. With a groan, I dragged her back up.

"I need to fuck you tonight, Mia."

Setting her back on the counter, I pushed her thighs wide and looked at her eyes. She wrapped her hands around my face and kissed me, her hunger equaling my own as I thrust inside her at once, catching her gasp in my mouth as her cunt stretched to accommodate me. I loved how fucking tight she was. Tight and hot, wet and willing.

She wrapped her legs around me, our bodies touching constantly as I fucked her, kissing her, feeling her tighten the grip of her legs around me, her mouth open for me as the walls of her pussy began to squeeze my cock. She said my name, closing her eyes as she came, and I just watched her, watched her face tense, her eyes soften, her grip tighten upon me, little whimpers coming from her throat as her pussy pulsed around my cock.

Once she loosened the lock of her legs, I set her down and turned her, leaning her over the counter and pushing her dress up to the middle of her back. I loved looking at her like this as she bent deep, thrusting her hips back and up. I gripped her buttocks and spread her open, my thumb closing over her asshole as I thrust once more into her drip-ping cunt, making her cry out. Gripping her hair with my other hand, I turned her head back and watched her face, watched her watch me, those pretty green eyes locked on mine as she came again, this time my cock throbbing inside her, emptying there, all while she watched, just as she had when all this had begun.

Spent, we remained on the floor in the kitchen of the café, both of us quiet, neither of us seeming to be able to get close enough to the other.

"Can you reach the cake?" Mia asked after a long while.

I chuckled and glanced at her, then reached up to take the serving dish that contained the last piece. "You're hungry?"

She shrugged a shoulder with an embarrassed look. "I like the cake."

I held it up to her and she bit off a piece. I did the same and we were once again silent as we ate that last piece of cake.

"I don't want to wait too long to get married," I said.

"Me either. I have no family or friends to invite, so we don't have to wait on anything."

"Now we'll be a family. You, me, and Gran — and who knows who else."

She lowered her lashes at that and I saw tears glistening in her eyes. "I may not be able to have babies ever, Julien. You have to know that." Her eyes searched mine. "You understand that, right?"

"I know. We have options. Adoption is something I'd like to explore at some point. Not quite yet, but in the future."

She nodded, but looked down at her lap.

With a finger under her chin, I forced her to meet my

gaze. "I love you, Mia. That's all. I don't care about anything else. I want a simple life with you, here. That's all."

A tear slipped from her eye, and I wiped it away.

"I love you too, and a simple life here is just what I want. I feel so very lucky already." She caressed my face and brushed her lips against mine in a soft kiss. "So very lucky."

The End

THANK YOU

Thank you for reading *Deviant!* I hope you enjoyed Julien and Mia's story. If you'd consider leaving a review at the store where you purchased this book, I would be so very grateful.

If you loved Deviant and want more, get to know the *Benedetti Mafia World* starting with Salvatore: a Dark Mafia Romance. Keep reading for a preview!

Make sure to sign up for my newsletter to stay updated on news and giveaways! You can find the link on my website: https://natasha-knight.com/subscribe/

Like my FB Author Page to keep updated on news and giveaways!

I have a FB Fan Group where I share exclusive teasers, give-aways and just fun stuff. Probably TMI :) It's called The Knight Spot. I'd love for you to join us!

SAMPLE FROM SALVATORE

A DARK MAFIA ROMANCE

I signed the contract before me, pressing so hard that the track of my signature left a groove on the sheet of paper. I set the pen down and slid the pages across the table to her.

Lucia.

I could barely meet her gaze as she raised big, innocent, frightened eyes to mine.

She looked at it, at the collected, official documents that would bind her to me. That would make her mine. I wasn't sure if she was reading or simply staring, trying to make sense of what had just happened. What had been decided for her. For both of us.

She turned reddened eyes to her father. I didn't miss the questions I saw inside them. The plea. The disbelief.

But DeMarco kept his eyes lowered, his head bent in defeat. He couldn't look at his daughter, not after what he'd been made to watch.

I understood that, and I hated my own father more for making him do it.

Lucia sucked in a ragged breath. Could everyone hear it or just me? I saw the rapid pulse beating in her neck. Her hand trembled when she picked up the pen. She met my gaze once more. One final plea? I watched her struggle against the tears that threatened to spill on her already stained cheeks.

I didn't know what I felt upon seeing them. Hell, I didn't know what I felt about anything at all anymore.

"Sign."

My father's command made her turn. I watched their gazes collide.

"We don't have all day."

To call him domineering was an understatement. He was someone who made grown men tremble.

But she didn't shy away.

"Sign, Lucia," her father said quietly.

She didn't look at anyone after that. Instead, she put pen to paper and signed her name—Lucia Annalisa DeMarco—on the dotted line adjacent to mine. My family's attorney applied the seal to the sheets as soon as she finished, quickly taking them and leaving the room.

I guess it was all official, then. Decided. Done.

My father stood, gave me his signature look of displeasure, and walked out of the room. Two of his men followed.

"Do you need a minute?" I asked her. Did she want to say good-bye to her father?

"No."

She refused to look at him or at me. Instead, she pushed her chair back and stood, the now-wrinkled white skirt falling over her thighs. She fisted her hands at her sides.

"I'm ready."

I rose and gestured to one of the waiting men. She walked ahead of him as if he walked her to her execution. I glanced at her father, then at the cold examining table with the leather restraints now hanging open, useless, their victim released. The image of what had happened there just moments earlier shamed me.

But it could have been so much worse for her.

It could have gone the way my father wanted. *His* cruelty knew no bounds.

She had me to thank for saving her from that.

So why did I still feel like a monster? A beast? A pathetic, spineless puppet?

I owned Lucia DeMarco, but the thought only made me sick. She was the token, the living, breathing trophy of my family's triumph over hers.

I walked out of the room and rode the elevator down to the lobby, emptying my eyes of emotion. That was one thing I did well.

I walked out onto the stifling, noisy Manhattan side-walk and climbed into the backseat of my waiting car. The driver knew where to take me, and twenty minutes later, I walked into the whorehouse, to a room in the back, the image of Lucia lying on that examining table, bound, struggling, her face turned away as the doctor probed her before declaring her intact, burned into my memory forever.

I'd stood beside her. I hadn't looked. Did that absolve me? Surely that meant something?

But why was my cock hard, then?

She'd cried quietly. I'd watched her tears slip off her face and fall to the floor and willed myself to be anywhere but there. Willed myself not to hear the sounds, my father's degrading words, her quiet breaths as she struggled to remain silent.

All while I'd stood by.

I was a coward. A monster. Because when I did finally meet those burning amber eyes, when I dared shift my gaze to hers, our eyes had locked, and I saw the quiet plea inside them. A silent cry for help.

In desperation, she'd sought *my* help.

And I'd looked away.

Her father's face had gone white when he'd realized the full cost he'd agreed to; the payment of the debt he'd set upon her shoulders.

Her life for his. For all of theirs.

Fucking selfish bastard didn't deserve to live. He should have died to protect her. He should never—ever—have allowed this to happen.

I sucked in a breath, heavy and wet, drowning me.

I poured myself a drink, slammed it back, and repeated. Whiskey was good. Whiskey dulled the scene replaying in my head. But it did nothing to wipe out the image of her eyes on mine. Her terrified, desperate eyes.

I threw the glass, smashing it in the corner. One of the whores came to me, knelt between my spread legs, and took my cock out of my pants. Her lips moved, saying something I didn't hear over the war raging inside my head, and fucked up as fucked up can be, she took my already hard cock into her mouth.

I gripped a handful of the bitch's hair and closed my eyes, letting her do her work, taking me deep into her throat. But I didn't want gentle, not now. I needed more. I stood, squeezed my eyes shut against the image of Lucia on that table, and fucked the whore's face until she choked and tears streamed down her cheeks. Until I finally came, emptying down her throat, the sexual release, like the whiskey, gave me nothing. There wasn't enough sex or alcohol in the world to burn that particular image of Lucia out of my mind, but maybe I deserved it. Deserved the guilt.

I should man up and own it. I allowed it all to happen, after all. I stood by and did nothing.

And now, she was mine, and I was hers.

Her very own monster.

Available in all stores!

ALSO BY NATASHA KNIGHT

Dark Legacy Duet

Taken (Dark Legacy Duet, Book 1)

Torn (Dark Legacy Duet, Book 2)

Benedetti Mafia World

Salvatore: a Dark Mafia Romance

Dominic: a Dark Mafia Romance

Sergio: a Dark Mafia Romance

The Benedetti Brothers Duet

Captive Beauty

Giovanni

The Amado Brothers

Dishonorable

Disgraced

Unhinged

Standalone Dark Romance

Deviant

Beautiful Liar

Retribution

Theirs To Take

Captive, Mine

Alpha

Given to the Savage

Taken by the Beast

Claimed by the Beast

Captive's Desire

Protective Custody

Amy's Strict Doctor

Taming Emma

Taming Megan

Taming Naia

Reclaiming Sophie

The Firefighter's Girl

Dangerous Defiance

Her Rogue Knight

Taught To Kneel

Tamed: the Roark Brothers Trilogy

ABOUT THE AUTHOR

USA Today bestselling author of contemporary romance, Natasha Knight specializes in dark, tortured heroes. Happily-Ever-Afters are guaranteed, but she likes to put her characters through hell to get them there. She's evil like that.

Want more?
www.natasha-knight.com
natasha-knight@outlook.com

Printed in Great Britain
by Amazon